Caramel Drizzle

LITTLE CAKES, BOOK FOURTEEN

PEPPER NORTH

PAIGE MICHAELS

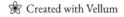

About the Book

Welcome to Little Cakes, the bakery that plays Daddy matchmaker! Little Cakes is a sweet and satisfying series, but dare to taste only if you like delicious Daddies, luscious Littles, and guaranteed happily-ever-afters.

Can a hardware store crush provide the building blocks for a happily-ever-after?

Jordi Cross is thrilled when she lands a new remodeling job. Sure, it's not a luxurious mansion or a fancy restaurant, but funky strip mall beauty shops deserve to be both gorgeous and functional, too. However, it turns out trying to build the hair-dressers' stations by herself was not her smartest move.

Callen James's hardware store has everything a contractor could need. If only he could stock someone special to make his life complete. One gorgeous and knowledgeable woman wiping out his supply of mini light bulbs and ordering tons of paint is defi-nitely as close as he's come to finding love in a long time, so of course he volunteers to deliver the supplies to her job site. As

Callen gets to know Jordi, it quickly becomes clear to him that the salon isn't the only thing in need of a Little TLC.

Chapter One

Clutching the list of supplies in her hand, Jordi walked into the new hardware store with determination and pure excitement coursing through her veins. With the office remodel of Valerie and Grayson behind her, she had just accepted a job to remodel an empty space, turning it into a new home for a hair salon. To her delight, the new supply depot she'd used for Valerie's job was even closer and more convenient to get to. Jordi crossed her fingers, hoping they would have just the things she needed for this specialized job.

"Hi."

The deep, rich voice made her look up in surprise to meet the eyes of a handsome man behind the large desk at the entrance. She stared at him for exactly two seconds longer than socially acceptable before shaking herself mentally to recover.

"Hi. You're not Ellen," she observed and then immediately wanted those words back.

"You're right. I'm Callen. Ellen is off for a school field trip with her kiddos today. Perhaps I can help you?"

"Oh. Maybe." Jordi stared at him, unable to rip her mind away from the burning question of whether his eyes really were that blue.

"Is that a list of supplies in your hand?" he probed gently.

"Oh, yes." Jordi looked down at the crumpled paper in her hand.

"Could I see it?" Callen asked kindly without a trace of amusement.

"Oh, yes!" Jordi realized she sounded like an idiot. Wanting to just dash out the doorway, she forced herself to walk forward. "I'm remodeling a hair salon. I'm sure you have everything here except maybe the mini lights for the stations."

"I'll be glad to order anything I don't have on hand," he assured her, taking the list as she thrust it forward. His fingers brushed over hers with the briefest contact but that was enough to make her shiver.

"Sorry, I keep it cool in here to give everyone a break from the heat," he apologized.

"It feels good," she responded in a rush, hoping he'd assume her beaded nipples under her polo shirt were due to the temperature in the store and not the fact that her body seemed to be going as crazy as her mind was.

Callen smiled at her and turned his attention to her list. His finger tapped on the top corner. "You're J. Cross. I was hoping to meet you. Thank you for shopping here. You were one of our first commercial contractors. It's tough to get people to switch to a new store."

"You're very convenient for me," Jordi said. *Wait. Did that sound funny?* She should have worded that differently.

"I'm glad. I'll take any reason for someone to walk in for that first job. Then it's up to me to keep you coming back." He looked down at the list. "I've got most of this in stock now. The rest I can have by tomorrow if you need it or next week if you want the lowest price."

"Next week is fine on the bulbs. I need the lumber and nails most today. Could someone load thirty two-by-fours on a cart for me while I go pick out some boxes?"

"Pull to the back after you've checked out. I'll have the guys load your truck for you," Callen directed. "If you need any help, please let me know. My goal is to be the most helpful hardware store in the city."

"Ellen is a gem," Jordi said, pulling herself together enough to praise the woman she'd worked with several times.

"She is. I'll get the rest of this ordered for you and we'll hold it in the back under your name. Want me to deliver it when it's all in?"

The thought of this man visiting her at her worksite made her blink a few times, but Jordi rallied and forced herself to concentrate. "That would be great. I think Ellen has my number on file. I can give you the salon's location."

"It's not the one over there by that cupcake bakery, Little Cakes, is it?"

"It is. You don't eat cupcakes," she blurted, looking over his muscular form. No one got that cut eating frosting.

"You've discovered my secret weakness. Don't tell anyone but the new Caramel Drizzle cupcakes Ellie is featuring now are the best ever!" His eyes twinkled at her in merriment.

"I... I'll have to try that flavor. Um, thanks... I'll get out of your hair and go get nailed... I mean pick up some nails," she corrected. *Just stop talking!*

"Aisle ten," he suggested with a grin.

What is wrong with you? Jordi mentally kicked herself as she hurried away.

Even though she told herself not to look, Callen wasn't at the desk when she went to the front to check out. Torn between being glad she could escape without making a bigger fool of herself and sad she didn't get to see him again, Jordi juggled the boxes of heavy nails as she waited in line.

"Here, set those down."

She turned at the sound of that voice. Callen stood behind her with a cart. Gratefully, she set down the boxes. "Thanks. That sale was too tempting."

"Just what I want to hear. I'll call you soon," he promised before moving away.

When he leaned over to pick up a squeegee that had fallen off the display, she reined in her desire to take a photo of his ass. No one would notice, right?

"Ma'am? I'm ready to check you out," the cashier called.

Jordi whipped her head around to find a huge space between her and the cash register. She'd totally missed that the person before her had finished and left. "Sorry. I don't know where my head is today," Jordi apologized as she pushed the cart forward.

Thank goodness I don't have a Daddy to spank me for lying.

Jordi pushed the image of Callen from her mind as she stacked boxes of nails on the counter. *Get a grip!*

Two days later, she assembled the framework of the beauty stations in the empty space. The owners of Shear Beauty had decided to move to the popular shopping area when a store front became available. Jordi loved the big open area and planned all sorts of magical touches. The stations were the first step. Once she got these done and wired, she'd have it made—a few coats of paint and lots of lightbulbs.

She'd hired a helper for the day, but he'd sent her a last-minute message that his daughter had come down with the flu. Jordi mustered on, sure she could figure out how to hold the heavy pieces in place to secure them. The first one was a challenge. Her muscles were screaming now as she lifted the back of the third into place on the base.

"Whoa! Let me help!"

That distinctive voice made her head jerk upward. "Callen?" She tried to look around the bulky piece to see him but it was too big.

"It's me. Here." Callen easily hefted the back and slid it into place. "Go ahead and secure it."

"Crap! I'm sorry," Jordi apologized as she forced herself to move and stop gawking at him. Quickly, she nailed the two pieces together.

"I surprised you," he said with a chuckle before looking around. "How many of these do you have to do?"

"Twelve. That was number three. Thanks."

"You should have some help hauling these around," he suggested.

A spark of indignation lit inside her. Handsome muscleman thought he needed to explain things to the dainty woman. "You're absolutely right. If it wasn't for the flu, my assistant would be here today. But since you can't leave a baby girl with a fever, he's not here, and I'm figuring it out."

"Of course you are," he said without missing a beat as if he had confidence in her. "I've got your supplies. No one will tell the boss if I'm a bit late getting back to the store. I'll help you get these lifted into place."

She cocked her head to one side. "Aren't you the boss?"

He winked. "Yep."

Jordi was about to refuse his help, but after following him out to his truck, she realized there was no way she could carry it all herself, and they quickly unloaded the mass of decorator lightbulbs along with the rest of her list.

When they were finished, he walked to the stack of display pieces. "Shall we start here?"

"It's not necessary," she repeated quickly, trying to keep herself from admitting she needed some muscle power.

"I know. I want to help. I never get to actually put things together anymore. Running a hardware store is like having a jumbo puzzle that you know will be spectacular, but you can't ever put it together. The pieces are all there, but someone else gets to have the fun."

She stared at him and understood completely. Jordi had wanted to be in the construction class at school but her female counselor had refused to okay it. Thank goodness the teacher of that class had had four daughters and believed Jordi should be permitted to do anything the boys were doing. When she'd gathered her courage to beg him to let her enroll in the class, he'd gone straight to the principal and secured her spot. Jordi had lived in his classroom for the last three years of her high school career. He'd taught her the curriculum and so much more. He'd done more for her than he would ever know. At the time, her home life hadn't been fantastic, and having someplace to be after school where someone cared about her and supported her had meant the world.

"Sorry for the attitude. Some men think women can't do this job. I shouldn't have lumped you in that group. I could use some help," she confessed, rubbing her shoulder.

"Did you hurt yourself?" he asked, moving forward to take her arm and rotate it gently around as if he were testing her range of motion.

Jordi stared at him as he touched her. When he paused to check her expression for any sign of pain, she assured him, "I'm okay. Really."

"Good. Let's get these knocked out for you." Callen patted her shoulder before turning his attention to the wood framework. He looked back at her expectantly, and she grabbed her hammer and rushed forward.

It took some time. Callen didn't hurry or show any signs of impatience. He simply hoisted the pieces into place and steadied them as she attached the pieces together. When he released the last one, she couldn't help celebrating.

"Woohoooo!" Jordi raised her hands over her head and danced in a circle. Hearing his chuckle, she froze in place. "Oops, sorry. I mean, thank you!"

"You're welcome, Little girl. I'll get back to the store. Maybe next time, you'll show me how to do a celebration dance. I think I need this in my life."

As she watched him walk away, trying not to focus on that tight, muscular butt, Jordi replayed his words.

Did he just call me Little girl?

Chapter Two

By the end of the next day, Jordi's eyes were almost crossed from wiring all the small lightbulbs into the stations. Rubbing her hands over her eyelids, she decided she needed a break before she connected more. Jordi looked out the window to see someone walk by with a box emblazoned with the cute Little Cakes logo. *A cupcake.*

"Time for a break," she announced to the waiting lights.

When they didn't answer, she took off her work belt and dropped it to the floor. Jordi locked the door carefully behind her. She had a big investment in tools, so she didn't want to walk away from them without securing the store.

With that task finished, she followed the covered walkway. Two stores away, she caught a whiff of vanilla, sugar, and chocolate. Congratulating herself on this really good idea, Jordi walked a bit faster. She reached for the door handle just as a large, callused hand encircled it.

"Oops! Sorry," she said, automatically stepping back to allow the other customer to go in first. Her eyes followed the trail of the attractive male form past broad shoulders to...

"After you."

"Callen?"

"We must have had the same idea. Cupcakes for the win. Allow me to treat you," he suggested with a broad smile.

Is he glad to see me?

"Oh, that's not necessary," she protested before wincing as she realized she said that to him a lot.

"I insist. Come on. Cupcakes are more fun if you have someone to enjoy them with." Callen waved her inside before him.

"Hi! Welcome to Little Cakes," the attractive, curvy brunette called out.

Their voices blended together perfectly as they greeted her in unplanned unison, "Hi, Ellie!"

"Jinx?" Jordi said without thinking.

When he laughed, she apologized. "Sorry. I grew up with brothers. I take it back."

He shook his head and guided her to the ordering line with his lips firmly sealed together. Callen definitely knew the rules to this game.

"Hi, guys! What can I get you? The special is Caramel Drizzle. Want to try one, Jordi? I know Callen's almost eaten his own weight in this flavor. It's his favorite."

Callen nodded eagerly and held up two fingers before waving a hand across his throat.

"Aww! You can't talk? Did she jinx you?" Ellie asked, quickly deducing what had happened.

"I didn't mean to... It just slipped out. I told him not to worry about it," Jordi said quickly.

"That doesn't work. You have to say their full name," Ellie reminded her.

"I know." Jordi gritted her teeth and jerked her head slightly at Callen.

"Oh, you don't know it. Callen will help you," Ellie assured her.

The delightful cupcake baker chatted easily with the pair as she dished up their cupcakes on plates and got them cups of water. Jordi tried to argue about Callen paying but it was hard to debate anything with a man who wouldn't speak. Finally, he carried their tray over to a window seat and waved her into a seat.

"Callen. This is ridiculous. Start talking," she said weakly.

He shook his head and pulled out a business card. Grabbing a pen from his pocket, he added something and handed it to her with a flourish.

"Callen Anthony James?"

"Whew! That's better!" he said. "I haven't been jinxed for a long time."

"Sorry, I had three brothers. It was automatic."

"Three younger sisters. They loved doing that to me," he shared.

"You were the only boy?" Jordi asked in fascination of their opposite childhoods.

"Yes, and I bet you were the youngest and only girl."

"Tomboy, through and through," she confessed as she nodded.

They looked at each other in silence for a moment. Jordi realized she was still holding his card. "Sorry. Here!" She tried to hand it back.

"Keep it. How else can you free me from the dreaded jinx?" he teased. "Besides, it has my cell phone on it. Call me if you need help with anything."

"Oh, I wouldn't impose..." she began and snapped her mouth closed at the stern look he gave her.

Watch out! Daddy alert!

Where did that come from? She'd been reading too many of those books. Daddies didn't really exist, did they? Jordi had run his use of *Little girl* over in her head for hours before deciding he must have said it simply because she was smaller than him. Like anyone wouldn't be smaller than him.

Pulling her thoughts together, Jordi waved the card and put it in her back pocket. "Got it. Thanks."

"Any time. Dive into a cupcake. I can't wait to see if you love them as much as I do," Callen urged.

Trying to use manners and be neat, Jordi peeled back the wrapper and picked up her fork as he watched. She slid the tines through the rich frosting drizzled with caramel and into the dense moist cake. *Damn.* Popping it into her mouth, she closed her eyes in ecstasy at the incredible flavor.

"I know, right?" Callen said, taking his wrapper off completely and lifting the cupcake to his mouth to take an immense bite.

Half the cupcake just disappeared!

"Mmm, these are so good. It's the caramel that really sets them apart. Ellie makes it herself. Not that chemical-flavored stuff you get at the grocery store."

"You know your caramel," she observed, trying to hide her smile.

"After you've jinxed someone, you're not allowed to smirk at them for at least an hour," he advised.

"That's like a rule?" she asked.

"Not one of the majorly important ones," he admitted.

"Are you a Daddy?" burst from her lips. Immediately, she felt her face heat, and she jumped to her feet. How had she just asked that?

His hand wrapped gently but firmly around her upper arm, keeping her from running away. "I am. You know that just as I know you're a Little girl. *My* Little, if I'm right."

Jordi sank back to sit in her chair. "You think I'm your Little girl?"

"I do. Something told me that the first time I saw you. Why do you think I came to deliver your order myself? I needed to see you again."

The hand wrapped around her arm loosened, and his thumb caressed her skin. She shivered from the sensation. *That feels way too good.*

"This is a lot to take in."

"Have a bite of cupcake and just let things happen. I promise I'm a good guy."

"I'll vouch for you being a good guy," Ellie said, startling them.

Callen dropped his hand as he turned to look at the baker. Jordi missed it instantly.

"I will say sometimes he's a smelly guy when he and Davis from Fitness Haven get into a sprint competition."

"Oh, you work out at the gym. That's how you found Little Cakes," Jordi said, fitting the bits of information together.

"I do. How did you discover the bakery?" Callen asked.

"I fixed some shelving in Design Magic for Gemma. I'd missed dinner and came in here for an energy boost," Jordi admitted.

"She's tried a different cupcake each time. I haven't hooked her on one flavor yet," Ellie shared.

"They're all so good. How do you know what the best is if you don't try everything?"

"What do you think of Caramel Drizzle?" Ellie probed.

"It's the best yet. There's something about the caramel..." Jordi peeked over at Callen. When he winked at her, she grinned back.

"I'll leave you two alone. Wave if you need anything," Ellie urged as she drifted away, cleaning tables and straightening the shop.

Silence fell over their table. It was easy and comfortable. Jordi took another bite of her cupcake to give herself time to enjoy the feeling of being with him.

The shrill tone of Callen's phone made her jump. He excused himself and answered, talking in short monosyllables that ended with "I'll be right there."

"Sorry, there's a problem at the shop. Will you call my number so I'll have yours in my phone?" he requested, reaching out to run his hand down her arm in a caress that reassured her he was totally into her. "We need to coordinate our schedules so we can get together."

"Okay," she promised.

Callen stood. With a wink, he popped the rest of his cupcake into his mouth and jogged out of the bakery.

She watched him go and tried not to stare. *My Daddy is hot!*

Instantly her brain went to work trying to convince her that somehow she'd misunderstood their conversation or that he couldn't really be interested in her. Were there trolls that pretended they were Daddies?

Of course there are. I'll be careful.

Jordi pulled the card out of her pocket and punched in the number. It rang twice and that voice answered.

"Thank you, Jordi."

"Thank you for the cupcake."

Feeling awkward, she disconnected the call and took another bite of the delicious cupcake in front of her. Her phone buzzed a short time later and she read the message on the screen.

You're welcome, Little girl.

She knew he'd waited to be safe to answer. *That's so Daddy.*

Chapter Three

Two women rapped on the big glass window the next morning. Recognizing the older woman, Jordi smiled and unlocked the door. "Hi, Louisa. You couldn't stay away, huh?"

"Hi, Jordi. Those mirrored stations look amazing," Louisa complimented. "I had a feeling when you said you'd design them yourself that we'd end up with something incredible, but those are fantastic!"

"I'm glad you like them. I was just testing out the lighting," Jordi said.

"I can't wait to see the final result!" the younger woman exclaimed before extending her hand to Jordi. "Hi, I'm Kiki, one of the hairdressers. I came to scope out a station."

"Hi, Kiki. I'm Jordi."

"You did not come to see what it looked like in here," Louisa protested with her hands on her hips. "Someone is addicted to that cupcake bakery. It's going to be dangerous working here."

"Fudge Crunch is the bomb," Kiki stated firmly.

"I like that one," Jordi admitted. "But I tried Caramel Drizzle last night. It tops that one in flavor."

"Take that back. It does not," Kiki countered in mock protest.

"You two are just making me hungry," Louisa remarked. "I heard you had a question for me?"

"Yes. Thanks for coming over."

Jordi led them to a storage area. "I can put doors on these shelves or not. It looks neater to have everything hidden, but it's easier to grab supplies if you don't have to stop and open a door each time. I had the idea to put doors on the first two set of cabinets. Clients can see those from the salon, but the others..."

"Leave them off," Kiki said emphatically.

"I think you have your answer. I'll run it past the owner since she's paying for everything, but that would be my choice, too," Louisa confided. "I'll send a text this afternoon. I like the way you think. Having a female contractor was a very smart idea. Our brains just work differently."

"Amen," Kiki echoed.

Jordi watched Kiki rub her bottom lightly with one hand. The look on her face was a combination of ouch and yum. *She looks like she's been spanked. Spanked? Is she Little, too? How many of us are there?*

"Jordi? Are you with us?" Louisa asked before glancing at Kiki. "I bet she's thinking of something else that's going to make our lives easier."

Tearing herself away from her thoughts, Jordi said quickly, "I'm always trying to make everyone's life easier. That keeps me in business. One more question. The design calls for towels to be in lower cabinets on the floor. Would it be easier if those cabinets were raised?"

"Up is better! My back will complain if I keep having to lean over four hundred times a day to get towels from the lowest shelf," Kiki declared.

"I agree. I'll add that one to my list to check on but that will help with cleaning, too. So it sounds like a win-win situation." Louisa made some notes in her phone. "Anything else?"

"No, those were the two I'd thought of. Feel free to look around. Be careful, there's a lot of equipment and supplies," Jordi warned.

The women walked around admiring different features Jordi had included in the design as she continued to work. A few minutes later, she noticed Louisa ruffling through a bunch of papers in a file that must have come from her large purse. The two women pored over them and then looked back at Jordi.

"Is there a problem?" Jordi asked, trying to appear unruffled while her entire body was in panic mode. *Please let everything be okay!*

"I just noticed it looks like you're setting up the plumbing for the shampoo bowls to be here. We moved them toward the rear of the store. The new chairs the owner picked out are too large to fit in this space," Louisa said hesitantly.

"Let me get my file," Jordi said, trying to keep calm. A change like that would cost a ton in both money and supplies. She couldn't have forgotten, could she?

Returning with her own thick file, she ruffled through the pages. "What date is the page you're looking at?"

Louisa recited the information and Jordi found it easily. "Got it. I seem to remember that something else canceled that decision to move the shampoo chairs back there. Let me look."

Forcing herself not to panic or rush, Jordi thumbed through the pages. *Come on! Please!* She backed up a few sheets and found two stuck together. "Here it is. Three days after that, I reported that the plumbing could go through that section but would have to be external as that is a weight-bearing wall that couldn't be further drilled through."

Louisa searched for that page and nodded. "I've got it. There's a follow-up question from the owner a few hours later asking if the placement of the sinks could be widened in the original planned location to accommodate the larger chairs. It was approved by you, so I'm sure you're already on that."

Containing her dismay, Jordi turned a page and mentally kicked herself. "Yep. I've got it here. I'll make sure those chairs fit easily in that space."

"Perfect. Thanks, Jordi. We'll get out of your hair and say we combed through the place. That will give us time for a cupcake," Louisa said with a grin.

"Enjoy."

"Come to me, Fudge Crunch," Kiki called as she urged her boss toward the door.

"You might try Caramel Drizzle," Jordi suggested.

"Never!"

Jordi's phone rang twenty minutes later as she sat on her stepladder looking at the sink problem. Dragging it out of her back pocket, she grinned to see that the man she had entered into her phone as Mr. Nice Butt was calling. "Hello!" she answered sharply, tickled by the comical but oh-so-true label but too weirded out by the problem ahead of her.

"You sound like something's wrong," that amazing voice responded in concern.

"Just another day in the life of a remodeler," she answered, trying to conceal her panic.

"That sounds ominous. I've got the day off today. Need another set of hands?" Callen asked.

She squelched her first impulse to jump on the offer. Her budget was threadbare, and if she'd screwed things up as badly as she was afraid she had, Jordi would be lucky to pay herself for her own time.

"Nope. I'm good. Thank you for helping me with that construction job. I can't impose on you further."

"You're not imposing on me. I'd like to spend some time with you and know you have a schedule to keep. If I come help you, maybe you can get ahead enough to quit early tonight, and I could take you to dinner."

"I don't think that's going to happen today," she answered, now worried about the time schedule.

"Little girl, talk to me. What's going on? What's wrong?"

The concern in his voice prompted her to blurt, "I made a mistake, okay? I lost track of a change order. Now, I've got to figure out how to fix this and give them what they need at the lowest impact to my bottom line."

"I'm sorry, Jordi. I'll be glad to help. I bet we can get you back on track."

Jordi shook her head in the empty store. She wanted to do this on her own. It irked her to have to ask for help. She'd worked so hard to establish herself in a predominantly male field. "Look. I don't know what to say. I like you. But I want to do this myself."

"I get that, Jordi. I want to spend time with you. How about if I come do the boring stuff a third grader could do just to save you some time? That would free you up to attack this problem with less of a time crunch, and I get my Little girl fix."

Jordi looked around at all the odds and ends that needed to be finalized. It would be amazing to have them all disappear. "Um. I'd be a fool not to let you take some things off my plate if you're sure you don't mind doing busy work?"

"It will be fun. Thank you for letting me help. I understand how it is to start a business. I had a lot of help a few years back."

A knock sounded on the glass door, and she whirled around to see him looking in at her. Instantly, her free hand lifted to her hair to smooth over the wild strands floating everywhere. "You're already here?" she asked the phone.

"Come open the door, Jordi. I need a hug."

Without hesitating a second, she flew to the door and unlocked it. His arms closed around her, and he lifted her up against him. Automatically, Jordi wrapped her legs around his waist to plaster herself against him. Holding her close, he pressed a kiss against the curve of her neck as he locked the door.

"You okay?" he probed.

"Better now. Thanks for coming."

"I'll always be in your corner."

Nodding, Jordi pushed lightly against his chest. Callen loosened his grip slightly and allowed her to slide down his torso. She was sorry when her feet touched the floor. The feel of his hard body was memorable.

She inhaled sharply and exhaled to pull herself together. Waving at the troublesome wall, she explained, "I need to go work on the pipes over there. I'm afraid I'm going to have to tear out drywall and re-plumb the connections."

"Would it help to talk through the problem?"

"Maybe." Jordi took his hand and pulled him over to the troublesome location. "They need larger chairs so the sinks have to be separated more from each other. The pipe connections are at the wrong intervals."

"Hmmm. I was looking at some model kitchens the other day and exposed metal piping seems to be coming into fashion. Could you do something fancy with the piping and have them start here and flare out to connect?" he suggested.

Trying to visualize, Jordi picked up some pieces of copper piping, fit them together, and held it against the wall above the connections. "You mean like this? Using elbows to crook the pipes to the connections? That could be funky looking." Hope sprang into her heart. *Could that work?*

"Let me hold them, and you step back to see what you think," Callen proposed. He dropped a kiss on the top of her head before she stepped away.

"That looks amazing. I love it. So, I just need some fancy piping and connections." Her mind ran a thousand miles a minute. *It could work!*

"Need me to run over to the store and bring you some supplies?"

"No. I want to design this right. The sinks weren't on my to-do list today. I've got time to think about it. If you'll help me with other tasks, that will help me get ahead."

"Point me toward the first job," he said with a smile.

Within minutes, they were both focused on different tasks. She loved having company. Working by herself was great. Jordi didn't have to rely on anyone other than herself, and she did everything *her* way. But... she really liked having Callen there.

Chapter Four

Four hours later, Jordi stood in the middle of the salon, spinning in a slow circle, grinning. "I can't believe how much we got done. I can't thank you enough."

Callen caught her shoulders to stop her. "You're going to get dizzy, Little girl. Do you know how many times you spun around?"

She shook her head, feeling a bit off balance like he suggested. "Oops. I just wanted to be able to see it all. I wish I had eyes in the back of my head so I could always see every aspect of the space I'm working on at the same time."

Callen chuckled. "That would be cool. Maybe if we also had eyes in the sides of our head and some lower, like on our hips."

"Oh. I could fit a lot of eyes on my hips," she commented, glancing down.

Callen's gaze was narrowed when she looked back up. "Did you just insinuate your hips were too big?"

Jordi winced. "Uhhh. Just pointing out the facts."

He shook his head. "Nope. That's not a fact at all, and I don't want to hear you demeaning yourself, understood? Your body is perfect just the way it is."

She swallowed. He was serious. She felt all warm and tingly from his insistence too. *He thinks I'm perfect?*

She thought about how she looked right now. Her wispy, straight brown hair was in a high ponytail, even though several strands had escaped to hang around her face—as usual. She had on jeans, work boots, and a formless T-shirt with her Cross Remodeling logo on it.

As she thought further, she realized this was basically what she'd been wearing every time she'd seen Callen. And yet, he thought he was her Daddy?

She eyed him suspiciously, narrowing her gaze as her mind went haywire. Why was he here?

Jordi set her hands on his shoulders and tried to push away from him. He was crowding her as she started to doubt his motives. Maybe he was a spy for a competitor or secretly had his own remodeling business, and he was trying to steal her ideas. It had to be one of those things. Otherwise, who dedicated half their day to helping someone out for no compensation?

"Jordi..." he warned in his deep Daddy voice. Was he even a Daddy at all? Maybe he was an imposter.

She broke free and took a step back, looking anywhere but at the gorgeous man in front of her.

"What's going through that pretty head of yours, Little one? I don't think I like it."

She took another step back. "Thanks for helping me today. I'm sure I can manage from here." She needed to get rid of him and extricate herself from this situation before she got hurt.

Already, she could feel her Little side creeping to the surface, threatening to bring tears with it. Why did her darn Little have to be teary?

"Jordi... The point of me helping was so that you could get off earlier and I could spend some quality time with you. I'd like to take you to dinner. Talk to me. You look spooked."

She drew in a breath and forced herself to be brave. "I don't really know you. Maybe you're a bad guy who's spying on me."

She felt ridiculous as she blurted that last part. It sounded sillier out loud.

When she glanced at him, his brow was furrowed. "You're right. I probably came on pretty strong with you, Sunshine. I didn't mean to scare you though. Sometimes you meet someone, and you just know you're meant to be with them. That's what happened when I saw you. Now I feel like I want to spend all my free time with you. I want to get to know you. I want to make you laugh and find out who your Little is. I want to hold you when you're sad and help you solve problems when you're frustrated."

Jordi didn't move as she tried to absorb everything Callen said. He seemed genuine.

He didn't step closer to her as he continued. "I promise I'm a hardware store owner. Nothing more. Not a spy. I'm pretty good friends with some people you know, in fact. I could give you references." He offered a slight smile.

Jordi blew out a breath, causing wisps of hair to fly around her face before settling back against her cheeks. "I'm sorry. I just panicked. You seem too good to be true."

His smile grew. "Sometimes good things happen. I know you're one of those. Let me prove I'm a good thing for you. Let me take you to dinner."

She held his gaze for long seconds, wondering if she should take this leap. Take a chance. If he hurt her, he would hurt her badly, but she might as well throw all her cards on the table and see how he reacted now. Why pretend she was someone she wasn't for days or weeks only to have him cringe when he learned the truth.

Fortifying herself, she drew in a deep breath. "I don't want to go to dinner."

His shoulders dropped slightly. So did his expression.

She lifted her hands in front of her to wring them together. "The truth is when I get off work, I just like to go home where I can be Little. I can shut off the world

27

and switch my headspace and slide into my other persona."

His brows lifted. "Okay..."

She needed to say more, make sure he understood. "I'm a tomboy in my adult skin. With three older brothers, I didn't have much choice. I spent my childhood proving to them I could keep up and do all the same things as them. Now that I'm an adult and live alone, I can lock my door and re-create my childhood the way part of me wishes it had been."

A smile grew on Callen's face. "So your Little is girly?"

Jordi nodded. "That's why I don't want to go out for dinner. I'm exhausted from adulting. If you want to know who I really am, you'll have to come to my apartment and see for yourself. We can pick up pizza or make mac and cheese or chicken nuggets."

"I love that idea, Sunshine."

Jordi stared at him hard, making sure he wasn't a fake Daddy. She wished there was radar for that sort of thing—a tool you could use to hold up and determine if a man was just saying the things he thought he should say to get someone to show their vulnerability before he hurt them.

She set her hands on her hips and narrowed her gaze, forcing every bit of her adult to stay in the forefront. "If you're messing with me or you laugh at me, I will never forgive you."

Callen took a step toward her. "I bet you have one characteristic that carries over from your adult to your Little."

"I do?"

"Yep, your sunny disposition, Sunshine." He gave her a mock frown. "Or am I going to find out your Little is sour and angry and bratty?" he teased.

She giggled and shook her head at the ludicrous thought. "Not a chance. My Little is sweet and sunny and fun. But she's not a tomboy. She doesn't like to get dirty."

His grin grew huge. "I want to meet her. I'll pick up the pizza and meet you at your apartment." He pulled out his phone, tapped the screen, and handed it to her. "Can you type in your address for me, Sunshine?"

She took it and hesitated. "You're sure you're not an ax murderer, right?"

He chuckled. "Nope. If you want to call some people to vouch for me, I'm friends with Davis from Fitness Haven, Tarson from Little Cakes, Maniac from Maniac Tats... You want more?"

She shook her head. "You sure know a lot of people."

He smiled. "I know them from Blaze. Have you ever been to Blaze?"

She shook her head again. "I've heard of it, but I've never been brave enough to go there. I'm not really into BDSM or anything. I'm just Little."

"Well, Little girl, there are a lot of Littles who belong to Blaze. You'd be surprised how many people in this town are Little if you take a harder look."

Jordi gasped as she realized if the men he'd listed were Daddies... That meant the women they dated or were married to were probably Little. "Wait, I assumed Ellie from Little Cakes might be Little, but Daisy, Tatiana, and Sue?" After all, Tarson was with Daisy, Tatiana with Maniac, and Sue with Davis. She'd at least met all of them several times. It was impossible not to since they all had shops in the area.

Callen's smile grew larger. "Mmm." He wasn't giving her a committal response, but she was glad. It wouldn't be polite to out people. She had a lot to think about though.

"Will you give me an hour? I'm gross. I'd like to shower and change—my clothes and my headspace."

"I'd be happy to, Little one." Callen closed the distance between them and reached up to stroke her cheek. "See you in an hour."

Chapter Five

What was I thinking? What was I thinking? What was I thinking?

Jordi paced back and forth in the living room of her apartment, wondering why on Earth she'd suggested something so ludicrous. She'd never invited anyone over to see her Little side, let alone a Daddy, and certainly not a Daddy who thought he was *her* Daddy.

He couldn't be lying. He had too many local friends to be lying to her. She would have been a lot more skeptical if he'd said he just moved to town and knew no one. But he knew more people than she did, and it seemed he knew who was Little too.

Her mind was still processing the thought that so many people she'd met peripherally were probably Little. Not just Ellie at Little Cakes, but most of her employees too. And Daisy from Daisy's Blooms?

The last project Jordi had worked on was an office space for Valerie and Grayson. She'd wondered several times if the two of them were Daddy and Little. Now it seemed less farfetched.

Jordi nearly jumped out of her skin when a knock sounded at the door. She spun around to stare at it. *What was I think-*

ing? she repeated in her head. She couldn't do this. Let a man into her apartment? Let him see her Little?

Ever since she'd gotten home an hour ago, she'd been running around like crazy to get ready. She'd needed to do some cleaning first and then take a shower and then get dressed and then fix her hair. By the time she was finally ready about five minutes ago, she'd stopped in her tracks and doubted her judgment.

"Jordi?" Callen called through the door.

Shit. That was him. And of course it was him. She'd said one hour, and it had been one hour.

Glancing down at herself, she realized there was no way out of this and shuffled toward the door. She opened it only a few inches, hiding behind the heavy wood and peeking out the slit.

Callen stood there, holding a pizza box and smiling at her. "Hey, Sunshine. Are you going to let me in?"

"Uhhh..." She felt uncertain. Should she let him in? Duh. She had to now. She'd dug this hole. Now she needed to face the music.

Finally, she stepped back, opening the door farther, but remaining behind it.

Callen strode into her apartment and set the pizza down on the small kitchen table in her attached kitchen area. He turned around and looked at Jordi. "Are you going to shut the door, Little one?"

She was still behind it, feeling sillier by the minute. She felt foolish for a combination of reasons now. Partly because of how she was dressed. Partly because of the fact that she was hiding. Partly because her mind was playing all kinds of tricks on her as she hovered half in her Little space and half in her adult space. Okay, maybe not half and half.

Inching slowly forward, Jordi finally shut the door and turned around to face Callen. Do or die time.

Callen took a seat on her couch and reached out a hand.

"Come here, Sunshine." His voice was soft and gentle and kind. No judgment.

She shuffled toward him, more nervous than she'd ever been. She couldn't speak. Her throat was broken. When she got close enough, Callen spread his knees, took her hands, and set them on his thighs. He palmed her hips next. "You look so pretty, Little one. I love this dress. Is it your favorite?"

She nodded slowly.

"Is baby blue your favorite color?"

She nodded again as she glanced down once more as if she needed to remind herself she was wearing her pale blue princess dress. It was way too fancy for pizza with a man she barely knew. The skirt had piles of ruffles. She'd even put on white knee socks and black Mary Janes. Her hair was in long braids with blue ribbons at the ends.

"I think you make the perfect princess." He let his hands slide behind her to the small of her back and pulled her in closer. "I'm so proud of you for taking a chance on me and letting yourself be vulnerable. It warms my heart. You're precious."

She loved being this close to him. Loved the way he held her. She wanted to lean into him. She wanted him to hug her.

Maybe she did sway that direction because he said, "Do you need a hug, Sunshine?"

She nodded again and let her body fall against his chest.

Callen pulled her tight and rubbed her back.

She set her cheek on his shoulder. He smelled so good. He'd obviously gone home and showered too. His hair was damp. His shampoo was something masculine and outdoorsy. He'd shaved. His face was so smooth.

A sudden thought went through her mind—what would it feel like for him to rub his cheeks against her thighs? She flushed deeply as she tried to shake the thought away.

"Take some deep breaths, Little one," he encouraged. "I know there are a lot of big feelings running through your head.

It's okay. I've got you. You're the most perfect Little girl ever. I know it's hard to let your guard down and trust Daddy, but I won't let you down. My heart is beating hard for you."

She drew in another deep breath, reminding herself how good he smelled.

"Can I lift you onto my lap, Sunshine?"

She nodded yet again, aware she hadn't spoken a single word since he'd arrived.

Callen lifted her up and settled her on one knee with her legs between his. "There." He ran his hand down one of her braids. "I love these braids. You're very good at fixing them. Maybe one day soon you'll let Daddy do your hair."

She swallowed over a lump in her throat. There was nothing she wanted more in the world than for a real Daddy to take care of her. Fix her hair. Give her a bath. Feed her even. Was it possible Callen might really be that man?

"Do you like princesses?" he asked next, fingering the front of her poufy dress.

She nodded.

"I bet you have a lot of pretty princess dresses then, yeah?"

She nodded again.

"And movies. Do you have all the good princess movies?"

Another nod.

"I bet you've seen them a dozen times each."

And another nod.

"Let's see..." He looked up and down her body and then glanced around the room. "I bet you like to play in the age range of about a toddler."

How did he know that?

He smiled. "I see a sippy cup on your counter and pictures you've colored on your fridge."

Oh.

"What's two plus two?" he asked.

Confused, she blurted out, "Four." And then she slapped a hand over her mouth, realizing he'd tricked her into speaking.

He chuckled, and his entire body vibrated, making her bounce. "She speaks," he declared. "I wasn't sure if your Little spoke."

Jordi licked her lips. "She speaks," she whispered. "She's just nervous."

"Understandable. Is she shy too?"

Jordi shrugged. "I don't know." She'd never thought about it. She'd never tested it.

"Ah. You haven't exposed your Little to anyone before, have you?"

"No, Sir," she whispered.

"How about instead of Sir, you call me Daddy?"

"Daddy..." she said, trying it out. It sounded weird coming from her mouth. She'd only ever said that out loud when she was role playing with her dolls alone.

"So, what does your Little like to do when no one else is here? What does a typical evening look like?"

"Well, I usually come home and shower and I think that washes my adult down the drain," Jordi began.

Callen chuckled. "That sounds perfect. What a creative idea. Then what?"

"Then I get dressed in something that makes me feel pretty, make myself something easy for dinner, and color or do a puzzle while I watch cartoons or movies. Also..." She glanced at him, feeling uncertain about what she was about to say next.

He lifted a brow. "What else?"

"I like to sing along to the movies. I know all the songs by heart, but I don't have a good voice so I'm sure it sounds awful."

"I bet you have a great voice. I can't wait to hear you."

She shook her head. "I couldn't sing in front of you, silly Daddy."

Callen's smile spread. "I like the way that sounds, Little one."

"Silly?" she joked.

He laughed again. "Not that part, the other part."

She tapped her lips, pretending not to remember.

Callen tipped her back in his arms and tickled her right under the ribs.

Jordi giggled and squirmed. Her skirt rose up on her thighs, and when Callen stopped tickling her, he set his palm on her bare leg.

"I love the sound of you laughing," he said, his voice deeper than before.

Her breath hitched as he gripped her thigh. "I assume you've read a lot of books about age play and probably done some internet research, which means you have a vision in your head of the perfect Daddy."

She shrugged, not sure what he was alluding to.

"In your imagination, does the Daddy kiss you when you're in Little space? Or would you prefer he save the sexy times for when you're in your adult space?"

She swallowed hard and licked her lips. She felt pretty sure her answer wouldn't displease him. "He kisses me in my Little space," she whispered, praying he wouldn't think that was weird. It certainly had never actually happened. It was all in her head.

Callen lifted his hand from her thigh and brought it to her cheek. "How about if I kiss you? Maybe that would help break the ice."

"Okay." She wanted that more than anything, even if this relationship was moving rather fast.

Callen held her gaze while he slowly lowered his mouth to hers.

The moment their lips touched, fireworks went off in the room. Sparkly ones that danced in her peripheral vision as he nibbled on her mouth several times before deepening the kiss. He even tipped his head to one side and held hers right where he wanted it.

Jordi melted into him. The kiss was the best she'd ever had, and it had been a long time since anyone had kissed her. A very long time.

When he finally released her lips, he set his forehead against hers. They were both panting. "Wow," he said. "If there was any doubt you were mine, it's obliterated now."

She was breathing heavily as she held his gaze. She felt like she was in a dream. Surely this was too good to be true.

Chapter Six

Callen couldn't believe how well this was going. He could tell his Little girl was very nervous. She'd been so brave to dress up for him and let him see her true colors.

It was hard to believe this precious Little girl practiced her kink alone in her apartment, sharing it with no one. She wasn't even a member of Blaze.

The first time he'd set eyes on her had been the other day when she'd come into the hardware store while he happened to be working at the welcome desk. God bless Ellen for chaperoning her kid's school field trip that day.

Callen's main goal for this evening was to make Jordi feel comfortable and at ease as her Little in front of him. He needed to be careful not to let her feel self-conscious about anything.

"Best kiss ever," he declared.

She giggled. "You're just saying that."

He lifted his brows. "Daddy will never lie to you. Are you suggesting that kiss was just so-so or ordinary?" he teased.

She shook her head, causing her braids to fly around. "No, silly Daddy. It was the very best kiss." She bit her lower lip as a devious look took over her face before she spoke again. "I mean,

I think it was. It's been a while since I kissed someone. Maybe I just don't remember it that well."

He grabbed her waist and gave her another tickle, making her squirm delightfully on his knee. Did she have any idea how hard his cock was and had been since he'd stepped into her apartment?

He brought his lips to hers. "Maybe we should do it again so you can decide for sure?"

She gasped and nodded slightly. "I think that's the best idea. For research purposes, of course."

He groaned as he took her mouth again, kissing the sense out of her while she turned her torso more fully toward him and grabbed his shoulders.

When he broke free of her the second time, it was for self-preservation. He was close to losing his mind with lust, and kissing was as far as he was willing to let things go tonight.

"You're a very tempting Little girl, Jordi." He lowered his lips to her neck and kissed behind her ear, loving the way she shuddered before whispering into her delicate ear, "We should eat. The pizza is getting cold."

Before she could respond, Callen gripped under her bottom and rose to his feet to carry her across the room to the table.

She squealed. "Silly Daddy, you can't carry me."

He chuckled before he lowered her to one of the kitchen chairs. "Why not? I just did."

"I'm too big," she argued.

He gripped her chin and leaned in close. "You're just right. Nothing about you is too big. Besides, I work out." He rose to standing and held up one of his arms, flexing his muscle like Popeye. "See? Your Daddy's strong."

Did she start panting? Damn, she was cute. She even licked her lips. "I see that," she murmured.

Needing a bit of distance before he came in his jeans, Callen headed for her counter and grabbed the sippy cup. "What do you want to drink, Sunshine?"

"Can I have juice?"

Damn. Walking away from her was not going to fix his hard-on. Not if she was going to be all sweet and cute and adorable and ask him if she could have juice for dinner.

"Sure, Little one." He opened her fridge, found the apple juice, and took it out. "Do you usually dilute it, Sunshine?"

"Yes, silly Daddy."

He chuckled as he prepared it, and when he brought it to her, he held it out of reach and met her gaze. "I think you can call me Daddy now without the silly part." He knew adding the word silly had made it easier for her to call him Daddy so far, but he really wanted her to look him in the eye and call him Daddy outright.

Was he pushing her? He didn't think so. Even though he'd only been there half an hour, they'd moved mountains in that time. He knew a lot more about her, he'd tasted her lips for nearly half that time, and he hoped she was feeling more comfortable with him.

She hesitated and then drew in a deep breath. "May I have my juice please, Daddy?"

If there was any part of him that had held back, it melted and wrapped around her pinky at those words. He kissed her forehead and handed her the juice.

After pulling the pizza box closer, he opened it. "I wasn't sure what you liked, so I got half cheese and half everything. I figured it would work either way because I have a favorite way to eat pizza."

She looked up at him, cocked her head to one side, and giggled. "I like everything on my pizza. What way do you like to eat it?"

Callen reached over, picked up the cheese half, and folded it over the supreme half. "Like a sandwich," he declared as he broke apart what was now four giant slices with crust on both the top and the bottom.

She giggled again. "That's so creative. Then your fingers don't get all slippery from the grease."

"Exactly. But you do have to have a wide mouth. Is your mouth big enough for something this thick?"

She tipped her head back and opened her mouth really wide.

That was a mistake to ask. Callen ripped his mind away from the steamy place it had gone to immediately and forced himself to speak normally.

"Yep. It looks like you'll be able to do it." He strode back across the room using the cover provided by the kitchen to shift his heavy cock in his jeans. *Down, boy.* As he struggled to regain control, Callen opened two cabinets before finding her plates. After returning with them, he slid one double-decker slice onto a plate in front of her. "Try it. See if you can do it. If it's too messy or too hard to get your lips around, Daddy can cut it up into smaller pieces."

She looked at the slice for a moment and then at him again, cocking her head to the side. "And then what would happen?"

He thought about her question for a moment before realizing her intent. "Oh, well, several things could happen. It would depend on how young your Little is at the time. You could eat the smaller bites with your fingers, Daddy could feed you with a rubber-coated spork, or you could feed yourself."

Jordi grinned. "You don't have a preference?"

"Nope. I already know what I need to know, and that's that I'm your Daddy. The rest will work itself out. I'll take my cues from you as we figure out what age you like to be. Maybe you like to be different ages on different nights? I suspect you're not certain right now, and we'll feel it out together."

Callen slid two of the double slices onto his plate before heading to the sink to get a glass of water. When he sat back down, Jordi was still grinning. "Do all Daddies know just the right things to say?"

He smiled at her. "I don't know, Sunshine. I don't even

know if I will always know the right things to say, but I do know when you're attracted to someone the way I'm attracted to you, nothing they say sounds wrong."

"Mmm. Good point. You might be right. I guess I'm also attracted to you the same amount. I don't know the right answer to my question either. My head is all over the place trying to decide. I think I want to try all the ways. Tonight, I'll see if I can pick up the pizza and eat it folded over with my hands. Maybe the next time we have pizza you can cut it up and feed me. For research purposes, of course," she suggested.

"But of course. For research." He winked at her and took a huge bite.

Jordi did the same, leaning way over her plate, probably to avoid getting any of the grease on her dress.

"Do you have a bib, Sunshine?"

She nodded. "Yes, Daddy. In the drawer on the right. Can you get me one?"

He couldn't help but kiss her forehead again as he stood. Seconds later, he slid a dishtowel bib over her head and smoothed it down to protect her dress. "Perfect. Just like you."

Her cheeks turned bright red as she took another bite. She was grinning too. They were making headway. She'd come a long way since he'd first entered her apartment.

And Callen had never been more certain of anything in his life.

When they'd eaten all the pizza they could fit in their stomachs, Callen suggested, "Would you like to choose a movie to watch?"

"Sure. What do you like? Princesses and magic? Princesses and adventure? Princesses and adorable animals that make you want to hug them and kiss their faces over and over again?"

"I think I'd like to watch that last one," Callen selected, knowing immediately which one *she* wanted to watch from her descriptions.

"Really. Me, too. It's like you can read my mind," Jordi

cheered before she stopped to look at him with a worried expression. "You can't, can you?"

"Read your mind?"

"Yes. You'd tell me if you could, right?" Jordi watched his face carefully as if trying to judge his honesty.

"I can't read your mind, Little girl. Sometimes, I get hints about what you might be thinking from your expression, but your thoughts are your own unless you choose to share them."

"Oh, good," she said in a rush. "Would you like to color while we watch the movie? I could make you a picture for your fridge?"

"I would love to have a piece of original art by Jordi on my fridge. I love to color, too, but I'm not as good as you are. No judgment if I go outside the lines, okay?"

"Deal!" she agreed and dropped her voice to a confidential whisper. "I make an oopsie sometimes too. We'll just pretend it doesn't happen."

"I like that idea, Sunshine."

In just a few minutes, she had a movie playing for them with the necessary criteria and had selected a picture for him to color. It seemed like some of her skills in organizing jobs and making decisions extended to her free time as well.

When he picked up a purple crayon to color in his tomato, she shook her head, warning him that wasn't the right choice. "Thanks, Sunshine."

About ten minutes into the movie, she started swaying to the music and humming along. Callen took a chance and started to sing the words. Jordi froze and stared at him.

"Sing with me, Little girl," he urged and watched an enchanting blush spread across her face. He continued to sing, waiting for her to be brave. In a whisper-quiet voice, she joined him. He blinked at the beautiful tone of her voice but didn't allow himself to react. Slowly, she gained confidence and her volume increased. Callen had to fight himself not to stop singing from astonishment. Her voice wowed him with its range and appeal. He could have listened to her forever. Had he guessed why she didn't like to have others hear her sing, it wouldn't have been because her voice was too good.

When the song was over, he leaned over to kiss the top of her bent head. "I love hearing you sing. Thank you for being brave."

"It was fun to sing with you, Daddy."

"I enjoy singing with you. Do you know the next song?"

She nodded eagerly. "I can teach you," she offered.

"I'd love to learn." Trying to keep the stress on her singing low, he gestured back at the picture and picked up a pink crayon. "What do you think? Pink for the grass."

Jordi shook her head with a sad expression and picked up the green to hand to him. "Try this, Daddy. Here comes the song!"

Callen did his best to sing along with her and watched Jordi relax into her Littleness. She scooted closer to him as she sat on the floor in front of the coffee table until she could lean against his leg to watch TV. He smoothed his hand over her braids.

Too soon, a glance at the clock told him it was Jordi's bedtime. He didn't want to end their evening, but her yawns forced him to announce, "It's time to turn off the movie, Sunshine, and get ready for bed."

"But the movie's not over," she whined.

"I know, but you're tired. Note where we are in the movie and we'll finish it tomorrow," he directed firmly.

"You'll come back tomorrow?" she asked, perking up from the slouched position she'd sunk into when he'd announced that it was time to stop the movie.

"I will."

"Will you sing with me?" she asked.

"I would love to sing with you tomorrow. Bedtime." Callen picked up the remote and turned it off before carefully typing the time stamp of where they were in the movie in his phone. "Let's put the crayons away."

"I can do it tomorrow," she rushed to assure him.

"It's easier to clean up as we go. That way you don't have to run around tomorrow getting ready for me. See! All done."

After yawning widely, Jordi admitted, "All that singing made me tired."

"I know. Let's get you in bed. You've already taken a shower, so let's take off your princess dress and hang it up."

"Will you help me with the buttons?" she asked, turning around.

"Of course." Callen carefully released the fasteners, discovering she wore a sports bra and shorts under the fancy ruffles. He stood to boost Jordi onto her feet and slid the dress off her shoulders and down to the floor.

As she stepped out of the dress, Jordi shook it out carefully to smooth the wrinkles. "I hang them in the hall closet," she shared. "I don't get many guests, so I don't need a place to hang coats."

Callen followed her over and smiled when she opened the closet to find several princess dresses hanging together safely. Jordi sorted through them to find just the right place. With the dress carefully slid into place and straightened, Jordi ran her hand over the pretty rainbow-colored fabric and closed the door.

"Are you telling them goodnight, Little girl?" he asked, enchanted.

"Yes. All the princesses are my friends."

She needs some real Little friends. Callen set a goal of having a play date for Jordi. Just one Little girl to start. He'd figure out who later.

Cupping his hands over her shoulders, Callen guided Jordi down the hall to her bedroom. It looked like a disaster area—but an organized mess. Work clothes folded by the door. Stuffies piled carefully by the bed. And a stack of what had to be clean clothes dumped on top of the dresser.

"Um... Sorry. I didn't have time to clean in here," she said nervously.

"You have too many things to wrangle, don't you, Little girl?"

"I do. I'm so tired when I come home. Coloring and watching movies helps me relax so I can sleep and I'm ready to go back to work the next day," she confessed, focusing on her bare toes scuffing into the carpet instead of looking at him.

"Then, we come up with a plan. Daddies help Little girls with miscellaneous things that complicate their lives. Perhaps you'd allow me to take a few things off your to-do list?" he suggested.

"I don't want to impose on you," she answered, peeking up at him.

"I promise I won't do anything I don't want to do."

When she yawned, Callen knew she needed to go to bed. "What do you wear to sleep in?"

"My PJs. I keep them under my pillow," Jordi shared as she retrieved them. She held them tight against her chest and shifted back and forth.

"Are you ready for me to help you change into your PJs or would you like to take them with you when you potty and change in the bathroom?"

"Bathroom," she whispered.

"I think that's a good idea. Soon Daddy will help you, but for tonight, you can just model them for Daddy while he tucks you into bed. Go, Sunshine," he directed with a smile.

"Okay."

In a flash, she was gone. Callen picked up keys, measuring tape, pencil, and a few other odds and ends Jordi had obviously emptied out of her pockets when she'd gotten home from the worksite. He looked around the room and found a clear decorative jar on the dresser. *Perfect.*

With that organized, he turned back the covers and found a

well-loved stuffie. The flat tail and buck teeth clued Callen in immediately that this was a beaver. He grinned at the thought of his Little girl choosing an animal who builds things as her favorite.

"His name is Norwood. You're not going to make fun of me for sleeping with a stuffie, are you?"

"Of course not. I am very glad to meet Norwood. Come get into bed, Jordi."

He helped her slide into bed and pulled the covers over her pajamas. Tracing one pattern decorating the collar, he told her, "Saws cutting logs looks like the very best set of PJs for a Little girl who loves to work with her hands."

"I bought four pairs when I found them. I knew I'd probably never find them again."

"Smart! Now you've got backups."

"Only one more pair," she said sadly.

"Don't worry about running out yet. I bet we can find some more. If not, I bet we can find something you like just as well," he suggested, processing as he talked that he already planned to be there in the future.

"What are you smiling at?" she asked, tilting her head to the side.

"I'm happy to be here with you, Little girl. If you'll keep me, I'd like to be here for a very long time."

Jordi started to say something but closed her mouth. Instead, she just nodded.

"Time for lights out, Sunshine. Are you comfortable? Do you sleep on your back?"

When she shook her head, Callen urged her to make herself comfortable. Immediately, she curled up on her side with Norwood hugged close to her chest. He tucked the covers around her and leaned down to kiss her hair.

"Could I have a real kiss?" Jordi asked.

Callen answered her with a kiss that he'd wanted to give her all night long. When he lifted his head, she touched her lips with a look of wonder.

"Now that's a goodnight kiss," she blurted.

"Sweet dreams, Little girl. I'll see you tomorrow."

"Night, Daddy."

It took all that he had to turn and walk out of her bedroom, through the apartment, and to the door. Enabling the lock so it would be secure when he closed it after him, Callen let himself out quietly.

Chapter Seven

Starting her day at The Hardware & Lumber Spot, Jordi held her breath as she walked in. Callen wasn't at the front desk. He had more things to do than be the door greeter.

Sighing quietly, she headed toward the piping to get the supplies she needed to finish the modification for the sinks. As Jordi filled her cart, she pondered how she could support the weight of the sinks to attach them to the wall. Planning to stack boxes and lumber at the right height, she headed to the cash registers.

"Hi, Jordi."

Turning to spot Ellen, Jordi smiled and greeted the employee. "Hi, Ellen."

"Hi. Mr. James left something for you here at the desk." She walked around the desk and pulled out a fully assembled device. "I'm supposed to have a stockman put this in your truck for you. Here are the directions."

"I'm afraid that's not in my budget," Jordi said, without raising her hand to accept the booklet.

"It's already paid for and ready to go. It's a support for someone working alone." Ellen spotted the piping in Jordi's cart. "If you have heavy sinks to go with those pipes, you can adjust it to whatever height you need while you make the connections or allow the adhesive to cure."

"That's amazing. It's like having an extra pair of hands," Jordi said, reaching out for the booklet.

"Mr. James said to tell you he appreciated you being willing to test this out for the store."

"Test it out for the store? Oh, yes. Of course. I'm glad to give it a practice drive," Jordi said, thinking on her feet.

"You check out and I'll call an employee to help you get this loaded," Ellen said, walking back to the desk to lift the phone.

"Thanks, Ellen."

Can I accept this? It has to cost too much.

Jordi purchased everything in her cart, debating the entire time whether she should accept the gift or not. *I could just drive away. I could have forgotten. He'll never believe that.*

Her phone buzzed in her back pocket as she walked out to the truck. Juggling her keys and pushing the cart, Jordi found a text message.

Let me take care of you, Little girl.

She stared at the screen before shoving it back in her pocket. Jordi looked around to see if there were cameras in the parking lot and found several security ones. *Is he watching me?*

Quickly, she loaded all her supplies into the truck and jumped into the driver's seat. Feeling the phone in her back pocket, she pulled it out to avoid cracking the screen and found a new message.

Ellen just messaged me that you looked worried. I'm not watching you, Sunshine. This is a win-win. You get some help stabilizing things and I get to find out if this gadget actually works.

A sigh of relief escaped from her mouth. She'd been totally

ready to decide that Callen was a stalker even after last night. Jordi knew she needed some help. Her assistant had already called in for today and she really wanted to get those sinks in and test the fix Callen had suggested.

Before she could change her mind, Jordi texted back a relief emoji and her thanks.

Callen responded with a sun emoji.

Sunshine.

Grinning now, Jordi drove up to the pick-up zone and met a handsome employee who lifted the heavy device up easily into the back of her truck.

"Mr. James says be careful getting this out. Maybe back up to the store front to lower it down on the sidewalk. Then you can just wheel it inside."

"Thanks. That's a good idea."

When she arrived back at the shop and had the new machine inside, Jordi flopped down on a box to read the directions. Fiddling with it as she learned how to use the adjustable support, Jordi got excited. It didn't take long to devour the pamphlet.

Five hours later, she looked at the line of sinks spaced perfectly apart and the flourish of metal piping that added a unique flair. They were going to love it. She'd even coated the metal with a special protectant to make sure it didn't tarnish or spot. Part of her hated to leave it here. Jordi settled for taking a picture and started to clean up.

She almost had everything organized to work on the next item on her list when her phone rang. "Hello?"

"Hello, Sunshine. Did it work?"

"Hold on. Let me show you." Jordi lowered the phone to text him a picture of the finished project and one of her smiling.

She could hear his answers as he looked at the screen. "Nice! There's my sweet Little girl."

PEPPER NORTH & PAIGE MICHAELS

"Thank you again. That makes a world of difference."

"You are welcome. Want to come to Daddy's house for dinner tonight? You could bring Norwood and stay the night?" he suggested.

"Oh!" She paused a couple of seconds before adding, "Will I sleep with you?"

"I'd love to hold you in my arms all night, or you can sleep in your crib."

"I have a crib?"

"You do. I'll pick you and Norwood up at six."

"I think I'd rather drive to you. What's the address?" she requested.

"Of course. I'll text it to you,'" Callen promised. "See you at six." Her phone buzzed a minute later.

West Fortieth Street? She had no idea where that was. Pressing on the address, Jordi checked the GPS. It was on the edge of town about twenty minutes from her apartment.

Checking the time, Jordi threw herself back into the remaining tasks she wanted to accomplish before calling it a day. When she took a break to use the restroom, Jordi called up the address on a site that would give her a view from eye level.

"Oh!" Jordi was amazed at the beautiful house that filled the screen. *That looks like a Daddy house.*

Forcing herself to concentrate on one last task, she got sucked into the job. When she caught sight of the time on her phone, Jordi cursed and grabbed for her phone. Sending him a message saying she was almost on her way, she took time to clean up the area before jumping in the truck. There wasn't enough time to go home without being really late, so she drove right there.

A movement at the front of the house caught her attention, and she saw Callen stand to wave. He walked down from the front porch and indicated that she should pull into his driveway.

By the time she turned off the motor, Callen stood outside

her door. Opening it, he leaned in to give her a hug before unbuckling her seatbelt and scooping her out of the driver's seat. "I was worried you weren't coming."

He set her down on her feet and turned back toward the truck. He probably intended to grab her bag, but there was nothing in the cab. "Did you decide not to stay?"

"I lost track of time and rushed over here so I wouldn't be too late."

"Ah, gotcha. Come on in. We can figure everything out. I'm glad you're here. Are you hungry?"

"Yes." She let him take her hand and lead her toward the front door. Jordi hesitated at the sight of the long swing that still swayed on the porch. "You have a swing?"

"I do. Come sit down."

Eagerly, she took a place at one end so he could sit at the other. Callen sat next to her and wrapped an arm around her. He set the swing gently in motion by pushing with his feet.

"I love to sit out here at night and swing. Look at that sunset," he said, pointing toward the horizon.

The sky was streaked with bands of pink, yellow, blue, and purple. She leaned against his strength and looked at it in wonder. "I'd sleep out here," she whispered.

"The mosquitos would eat you alive after the sun goes down. It's almost over now. You arrived just in time to see it."

When the last of the pink bands faded away, Jordi heard the high-pitched buzz of an insect next to her ear. "They're here!"

"Quick! Let's escape!"

Dashing inside, Jordi couldn't help giggling as Callen slapped one of the bloodsuckers who'd managed to take a sip before they'd taken refuge inside.

"You! Laughing as your Daddy gets bitten," Callen growled playfully.

"Sorry, Daddy," Jordi said, slapping her hands over her mouth to keep her giggles inside.

"Give Daddy a kiss to make everything better," he requested as he wrapped his arms around her to pull her close.

Jordi melted against him as his mouth pressed against hers. Softly at first, wooing her to respond. When she did, he deepened the kiss and dipped inside to taste her. Jordi wrapped her arms around his neck to hold on as she wiggled as close as possible. They were both slightly breathless when he lifted his head.

"I'm very glad you're here. Hungry?" he asked, brushing the wisps of hair that escaped from her ponytail away.

"Starving."

"Let's get you fed."

Her Daddy guided her further inside. A delicious aroma filled the air, making her tummy growl. She forced herself to ignore it and looked around. The house was beautifully decorated but comfortable. It wasn't a stuffy place where you'd hate to sit down in case you wrinkled the couch. She could see all the way from the front door to the back of the house, now shrouded in growing darkness. *That has to be a freaking amazing view.*

Past the living room was a huge open kitchen with a big oak table and tall chairs drawn up to the counter. A smaller casual area filled the space in front of the windows. There, Jordi could imagine curling up against her Daddy on the cushy leather sectional and propping up her feet to watch a movie.

"You have a beautiful home, Daddy."

"It's missing one very important component," he told her with a serious expression.

"What? You could put in a window seat in that other room to watch the sunset without the mosquitos. I like that swing myself," she said quickly.

"I'm talking about you, Little girl. My house hasn't been a home. I needed to find my Little," he said with a smile and a squeeze to her hand.

"Oh." Swallowing hard, she forced herself to ask, "Are you sure you're my Daddy?"

"I'm sure. I bet you've worried today. It's hard to meet someone new and know they're important."

"Scary important," she echoed, nodding.

"Then it's up to me to reassure you. First up, dinner. A Little girl with an empty stomach needs to eat. Do you need to wash your hands and potty?"

When she nodded, he gestured down the hall. "First door on your right."

Jordi darted down the hall, needing to go badly now that he'd mentioned it. *Don't wet your pants! Don't wet your pants!* She made it to the restroom and after a frantic struggle with her pants, she collapsed to the seat.

When she returned, he had pulled something from the oven, making it smell even better. "What is that?"

"Come sit down and find out," Callen urged, guiding her with an arm around her waist toward the table. He pulled out a chair for her and helped Jordi sit. Without any fuss to make her feel self-conscious, her Daddy drew a bib over her head before brushing her hair from her face and dropping a kiss on her lips.

"Have a drink. I bet you're thirsty."

As he returned to the kitchen, she eagerly picked up the cute sippy cup and lifted it to her mouth, expecting to taste juice. To her delight, yummy chocolate milk filled her mouth and she wiggled happily in her seat. Yum!

"Taste good?" he asked.

"It's so good."

"I hope you like this as well," he said, carrying over a large casserole filled with chicken and noodles.

Jordi leaned in to inhale deeply before asking, "Did you make that?"

"I did. One of my grandmother's favorite recipes. I only make it for very important people. I hope you like it."

Callen put a healthy portion on her plate and set it in front of her. "It's hot. Let it cool for a minute."

When she picked up her fork to dive in immediately, he

pressed her hand back to the table. "Wait. You'll burn your mouth. Let's sing a song and when we're done, I bet the noodles will be the perfect temperature."

He sang one of the songs they'd enjoyed last night. Her Daddy didn't force her to sing, he invited her to join him with his obvious happiness to share the music with her. She whispered the next stanza along with him as she watched him place a giant portion on his plate before reaching for her glass and refilling it from an insulated pitcher next to him. Her voice gained confidence with every passing second as the beautiful sound filled the large open space.

When the last note died out, Callen lifted her hand still clutching the fork and kissed her knuckles. "See if it's okay now. A small bite."

Jordi stabbed one noodle and lifted it to her mouth. She pressed it against her lip to check the temperature and then devoured it. "It's so good!" she mumbled around the treat.

"Careful, don't talk with your mouth full. I'm glad you like it."

The conversation at the table was quiet for a few minutes as he let her fill her belly. When she slowed down, he spooned another portion on the far side of her plate to cool down and requested, "Tell me about that support. What did you like? What didn't you like?"

Distracted by their conversation, Jordi ate until she couldn't eat another bite. Setting her fork down with a click on her plate, she leaned back in her chair. "That was the best thing I've had in—forever!"

"Hooray! I'm so glad. Would you like any more?"

"No way. I'm going to pop," she said, poking her tummy.

"We don't want that. Would you like to watch a movie while I get everything cleaned up?"

"What time is it? I don't want to drive home too late," Jordi said, looking around for a clock.

"It's seven-thirty. What would you think of getting in my

hot tub in a bit? I could throw your clothes into the wash and you could still spend the night with Daddy."

"You have a hot tub?" she asked, sitting up straight before slumping with disappointment. "Oh, I don't have a bathing suit."

"No problem. You could wear one of my T-shirts if you want."

"That might work," Jordi said, perking up once again. "But Norwood is home all by himself."

"We'll go get him tomorrow and bring him back to join us."

After hesitating for a minute, she sent a mental message to her stuffie. *I'm okay. I'll make sure to bring you with me tomorrow.*

"I'm going to be here tomorrow?" she asked as she realized what she'd thought.

"I hope you'll stay with me often and soon always. I want to spend time with you, Little girl."

"I want to spend time with you, too," she whispered.

Callen pushed his chair back and lifted her onto his lap. Wrapping his arms around her, he held Jordi close and rocked slightly. When she relaxed against him, he kissed her temple.

"I need to shower before I get in the hot tub. I'm all dusty. I don't want to get that in the water," she suggested.

"Do you want to shower by yourself?" he asked, leaning back to meet her gaze.

She understood he would give her a shower if she was comfortable with that, but he was letting her set the pace. "Can I take a quick one by myself?"

"Of course. Let me show you the way and get you a T-shirt to wear."

Callen boosted Jordi to her feet and stood to take her hand. Leading her down the hallway, he showed her through the master bedroom and into the huge attached bath. Soon she was equipped with towels, body wash, and shampoo as well as a T-shirt to wear. With a kiss, he excused himself.

"Shouldn't I help you do the dishes?"

"Little girls don't do dishes. Take your shower and come join me. I'll get the hot tub warming."

Jordi stared at the empty doorway and wrapped her arms around herself in a big hug. *Can he be as amazing as he seems?* A faint sound of princess music drifted to her. He was singing one of her favorites as he did the dishes. With a big smile, she undressed.

Chapter Eight

Wrapped in his T-shirt, Jordi grabbed her pile of dirty clothes and walked down the hallway toward the kitchen. She hesitated at the doorway into the family room and saw him flipping through the channels on the TV. He stopped at a cartoon and set the remote down before turning to look toward the hallway.

"Hi, Sunshine. Do you feel better?" he asked.

"Hi. It's amazing how good clean feels," she answered, walking forward. "I don't mind getting dirty, but I love showers."

"Do you like baths?"

"Not really. I'd have to take a shower before filling the tub anyway," she said with a shrug.

"Does getting into the hot tub sounds good?"

"Sure, if you want to. I'll have to take another shower when I get out," she pointed out nervously. Her excuse sounded silly even to her own ears, but the thought of getting in the hot tub with him made her private parts get all tingly and she was afraid all she'd be able to do if he took off his shirt would be drool, and that would embarrass her.

"You don't have a preference?" he asked, studying her face.

"Hmmm. I think I'd like to relax in a hot tub. But I know it's a bunch of work." She was talking nonsense and feeling foolish.

"I think it will help your muscles relax. Let's go give it a try. If it doesn't work for you, we'll come in to shower and relax in front of the TV."

"Okay. I'll watch TV while you change," she suggested, perching on the edge of the sectional.

"My backyard is protected, Sunshine. I'll drop my clothes off on a chair."

"You're going to get in naked? Aren't you going to wear swimming trunks?" *What is wrong with you? Stop talking. Get in the hot tub with the sexy man.*

"I wasn't planning to, but I can if you'd rather I'm all covered up."

"No, you should be comfortable. I won't look," she said quickly.

"You can look, Little girl. It's okay if you're curious about your Daddy's body."

He wrapped an arm around her arm and escorted her toward a room off the side of the kitchen. "Let's get the washer started before we go out back. Can you drop your clothes in for Daddy?"

She did as he instructed and stepped back while he added soap and turned on the machine. It seemed so intimate doing her wash at his house.

"Ready?" Daddy led her to the back deck where the only light spilled through the kitchen windows. She was relieved to see that the backyard featured a high fence and a thick screen around the deck area. Carefully stepping into the warm water with his help, Jordi avoided flashing him and settled onto the bench on the other side.

Callen rotated the switch to start the bubbles and stepped back away from the tub to undress. The T-shirt swirled around her and she tugged it down, trying to tuck the extra fabric under her thighs. Jordi studiously avoided looking at him as she heard the rustle of clothing. She glanced up at the ceiling over the hot tub when she caught a glimpse of his muscular tushie as he sat down before rotating his legs inside.

Callen sighed deeply. "It feels so good to sit in the hot tub at the end of a long day."

Jordi might agree if she wasn't so nervous. The T-shirt wouldn't stay down under her butt, air kept getting up inside it to make it poof out, and every time she flattened it down, she could easily see her nipples through the now-transparent material. Not just their color, but that they were stiff.

"Sunshine, look at Daddy."

She lifted her gaze, trying to hold the shirt down, uncertain now if her goal should be to keep the air out of it or let it in. Both looked ridiculous.

"The shirt isn't working out well in the water, is it?"

She shrugged. "It's fine."

"Mmm. I'm trying to read you, Little one. I can feel your stress from all the way over here. You've been fiddling with the T-shirt since you got in, you're as far away from Daddy as you can get, and you're quiet. Tell me what's bothering you."

"I'm fine," she lied.

He narrowed his gaze. "Do you know what happens to Little girls who fib to their Daddies?"

Her breath hitched. "In books they get spanked," she whispered.

"The books are right on that issue. So, let's try again. Tell Daddy what's bothering you. I promise I won't be mad. Are you uncomfortable being naked with me? Last night you said your Little liked to be kissed, but that doesn't necessarily mean your Little likes to engage in other sexy times. Now I'm wondering if you'd rather Daddy didn't mix sex with age play. And that's fine. I just need you to tell me."

She shook her head before she could remind herself that she would have to follow that denial up with words. *Darn.* "It's not that."

"So, your Little doesn't mind sex."

She shook her head again. "I don't know. I've never tried it." She bit her lip hard and then released it. "The thing is that I haven't had sex in a long time, and I'm feeling uncertain and awkward, and I don't want you to think I'm inadequate or something."

Callen slowly leaned forward. "I could never think you're inadequate, Sunshine."

Jordi sighed deeply, finding the strength to speak her mind. It wasn't like she could go on and on forever not telling her Daddy what she was thinking. "So, what happened was that I realized I was Little a long time ago, and I..." Why was this so hard?

"And you what, Jordi?" he encouraged gently.

She drew in another fortifying breath. "I stopped dating because...well, because I didn't know any Daddies, and I couldn't see the purpose in dating men who weren't Daddies."

"That makes sense, Little one."

"So, the thing is that before that, before when I didn't know I was Little inside, I was dating vanilla guys. I was young too, and it was so boring, and the sex was...bad." She somehow managed to giggle and then quickly covered her mouth.

When she looked at her Daddy, he was smiling.

She lowered her hand and flattened the stupid shirt again to push out the bubbles. "I sound pitiful."

"Not at all. You sound like a woman who figured out what she wanted and didn't settle for less."

"It sounds much better when you put it that way, but see, I'm not going to be very good at sex because I never really figured it out when I was younger, and I don't want to disappoint you."

"Jordi, you could never disappoint me. Sex is something that's amazing when you're with the right person *because* you're with the right person. It can be disastrous and disappointing when you try to force yourself to enjoy it with the wrong man. I suspect a part of you knew you were interested in age play even before you had the words for it. That's why a vanilla relationship never felt right."

She held her shirt down, gripping part of it between her knees. "That sounds right."

"What do you feel when you're with me, Little one?"

She sat up straighter and licked her lips. "All the things. So many things. And it's kind of scary because I don't want to mess up. When I think about you, I get all tingly and stuff, and that's never happened before. And I want you to touch me in my special places. And I don't even know how to touch you to make you feel good too. And—"

Callen reached out a hand above the water. "Come here, Sunshine. You're so far away. I need to hold you."

She pushed off the side of the hot tub and rushed across toward him, letting her Daddy catch her and pull her into his arms.

There was no way to ignore the giant hard-on he had or how it brushed against her thigh as he spread his legs and hauled her between them.

Her breath hitched when his hands came to her bare butt cheeks and then slid up under the shirt. "Let's take this off, yeah?"

She nodded and lifted her arms so he could remove it.

Daddy tossed it onto the deck before lifting her by the hips. "Straddle me, Little one."

She did as he asked, more than aware of her breasts now hovering out of the water.

As she wrapped her legs around his waist, his erection settled against her sex.

"Sit still," he whispered against her ear.

She hadn't realized she was rubbing her pussy against his length until he spoke, and she stiffened.

He rubbed her back. "It's okay, Jordi. Don't panic. I just don't want to come like a teenager, which was about to happen in five seconds."

"Oh." Was that really a thing?

He chuckled. "I haven't had sex in a pretty long time either, Sunshine. It's not different for me. I'm a Daddy through and through. Dating women who aren't Littles doesn't appeal to me. Finding the right Little was where I put all my focus, right up until you walked into my hardware store and stole my heart."

Speaking of hearts, hers was going to beat right out of her chest. She grabbed his shoulders to steady herself. "I can't believe you're real," she admitted.

"Sometimes I can't believe you are either, Little one. I keep looking in my phone contacts to make sure there really is an entry for Jordi Cross and that the line under it says *My Little Girl*. When I see it I assume I have not imagined you." His smile made the corners of his eyes crinkle.

She intentionally wiggled against his erection, giving him a coy grin. "I've only ever had sex under the covers in a bed with me on the bottom and the guy on top just pushing into me. I never even had an orgasm until a few years ago when I bought a vibrator and figured it out myself."

He was grinning.

"Are you laughing at me?"

He shook his head. "No, Little one. Never. I would never laugh at you. I'm thinking of all the ways I'm going to teach you how good sex can be. All the positions. I'm thinking about how loud you're going to scream when I thrust my tongue into you and then my fingers."

She gasped. Probably her cheeks were hot pink, but the

darkness of the night was hiding them, right? "And will I get to make you scream too, Daddy?"

"Definitely. Maybe not scream, but you're already the best sex partner I've had, and that's just from a few kisses and now you straddling me with your unbelievably sexy body while you rub your hot pussy against my cock. It's heaven."

"Now you're just being silly."

He shook his head. "Nope. Truth. Daddies don't tell lies."

"I have an IUD," she announced before she could filter herself.

His hands trailed up and down her back before cupping her butt. "That's good for birth control, Little one, but you should never have sex with someone without seeing a clean bill of health from them."

She narrowed her gaze. "You said you haven't been with anyone in a while. Don't you go to the doctor yearly?"

"Yes. Of course. I got tested the last time I was there. The report is in my desk. Would you like to see it?"

"I have proof too. I could even pull it up on my phone. I think I can trust you. We shouldn't have sex if I don't. I don't think real Daddies tell lies." She lifted a brow in a silent question.

He groaned. "No, they do not." He gripped her butt cheeks, pulling them apart. "I hadn't planned on having sex with you tonight, Jordi. There are lots of things we could do without penetration if you want Daddy to touch you." He punctuated his words by sliding his fingers around her thighs and lifting her slightly so he could drag them through her slit.

Jordi moaned. It felt so good. Better than anything she'd ever felt. "Daddy..."

Suddenly, he stood, holding her by the thighs. He spun around and set her on the edge of the hot tub, exposing her entire body to the night air. She wasn't chilled, but her nipples were hard peaks from her growing arousal.

PEPPER NORTH & PAIGE MICHAELS

Callen grabbed her hips. "Spread your legs, Sunshine."

She parted her knees, wondering what he might do. Already this surpassed any experience she'd ever had.

When he lowered his face to her sex and circled her clit with his lips, she nearly shot off the edge of the hot tub. She would have if he hadn't been holding her down.

He thrust his tongue into her next, making her cry out. She grabbed onto his shoulders as he did things she'd only read about in books. She didn't even have girlfriends she'd ever discussed this kind of thing with, so she'd been left to wonder.

When was the last time she'd had an orgasm? She couldn't remember. It had been a while, and she'd believed she could only do so with her powerful vibrator. Not with a man, and certainly not with his mouth.

He hummed against her mound before flicking his tongue rapidly over her clit until she stiffened her legs and tipped her head back. She was going to come. Holy cow. She was really going to come.

Seconds after that thought, she slid over the edge, her body pulsing against his mouth as he suckled and licked. As the waves of her release slowed, so did the pressure from his lips until he finally eased back and released one of her thighs to wipe his mouth with his hand.

Jordi was panting, and she was pretty sure there was a silly grin on her face. When she started shivering, he lifted her back into the water, settled her sideways on his lap, and cradled her in his arms so that most of her was submerged under the warm water. Her Daddy hadn't gotten it too hot. He'd thought of everything.

"I think I like your hot tub," she whispered as she stared at his chest and played with the light sprinkling of hair.

He laughed, his body shaking. "You were pretty uncertain before we got in."

She shook her head. "No. I was uncertain about being naked with you, not your hot tub."

"Ah. Well, I'm glad you've changed your mind."

When she caught her breath, she sat taller and turned to face him. "Can I straddle you again, Daddy?"

He lifted his brows. "Only if you want to, Little one. You're under no obligation to take me inside you just because I tasted your sweet pussy. We can stop right now if you'd like. But, if you straddle me, I might not be able to keep from coming against you even if you don't move."

She gave him what she hoped was a wicked grin. "Oh, I plan to move." She scrambled to turn and set her feet on either side of his hips. Hovering above him, she continued, "I plan to move up and down."

He grabbed her hips, but he didn't stop her from lining her pussy up with his enormous length and thrusting down.

A loud moan filled the night air. It took a moment for her to realize it had come from her. His shaft was so much bigger than anything she remembered. He filled her so full.

She grabbed his shoulders and tipped her head back toward the sky, knowing her breasts were bobbing above the water. She'd never felt sexier.

Callen's hand gripped her back. "Jordi, you feel so damn good. As soon as you move, I'm going to come."

She lowered her gaze to his. "Then I'll just keep riding you until you get hard again."

His eyes widened.

She knew she shocked him, but she was also shocking herself. Who was she?

His smile grew. "Someone is a wildcat in bed."

"This isn't a bed," she teased.

He chuckled.

She lifted slowly up a few inches and then thrust back down.

This time the moan came from her Daddy. Definitely. It gave her the strength to do it again. She felt a strange sense of power on top of him like this. Incredibly feminine and alive.

Teasing him with her channel, she eased off and thrust back down several more times, pausing so long in between that he was panting. He even growled. But he didn't say a word. He let her play, and that meant everything to her.

"Getting close, Jordi," he said as he slid a hand around between them and found her clit.

She gasped. "Daddy..."

"Yes, Little one?" he teased. "Did you have something to say?" He rubbed her clit fast and hard, driving her to the edge. When she couldn't take it another second, the need so fierce that she was wound as tight as a top, she braced herself on her heels and lifted up and down on his erection over and over.

Callen never lost contact with her clit. He kept stroking it until she came, and the moment she cried out her orgasm, he followed right on her heels.

Her Daddy wrapped his arms tight around her, holding her chest against his, keeping himself deeply impaled while her channel pulsed around his thick length.

His lips came to hers a moment later, his hands at the back of her head. He kissed her as if he'd never get another chance. Deep and long, his tongue searching and licking and sucking and finding. Tasting her while she tasted him.

And then his mouth slid to her ear, and he nibbled around the edge, making her shiver before he spoke. "You're mine, Jordi Cross. My Little girl. My woman. My life."

She whimpered. She didn't have the strength to respond. How was he coherent enough to talk?

"Hottest sex of my life," he continued. "It was already the hottest before you came on my mouth and then rode my cock. Now it left the stratosphere."

She smiled against him. She couldn't believe she'd been bold enough to even discuss her fears and thoughts let alone act on them. Apparently she could orgasm with a man, and apparently there were Daddies out there who could make a Little girl's dreams come true.

As her mind stopped spinning and her breathing eased, worries slipped in unbidden.

You've only known him a few days.

You can't be sure he will even call you tomorrow.

Who has sex with a man on the second date?

Chapter Nine

"Jordi..." he warned as he eased her back so he could see her face.

He was still buried inside her where he'd like to stay forever.

"You stiffened on me. Tell me what you're thinking."

She shook her head. "Nothing, Daddy," she lied.

He narrowed his gaze. "You got spooked, didn't you, Little one?"

She didn't respond. Nor would she look at him.

He needed to be patient with her and let her process. A lot had just happened. It was reasonable that she would be a bit nervous. But he also needed her to know that Little girls who fibbed ended up with sore bottoms. He couldn't let that slide.

Hoping that if he took charge and helped her back into her Little space, she would relax, he made a decision. Because there was no doubt his Jordi had mostly left her Little space while she rode him.

That was fine. He didn't care if she needed to be in her adult mindset when they had sex. Everyone was different. He could respect that. But now she was vulnerable and needy and doubts were seeping in, so it was time for Daddy to help her back into her Little.

He rubbed her back. "Here's what we're going to do. We're going to get out of the hot tub. Daddy will dry you off so we don't traipse water through the house, and then Daddy will take you to the shower and wash off the chlorine. After that, I'm going to spank you to help you remember that it's not okay to lie to Daddy. When your punishment is over, we'll climb into bed, and I will hold you."

She whimpered, but she didn't protest.

He took that as a win and rose, lifting her off his cock as he stood. That part sucked. He really liked being inside her. He hoped to do so a lot more in the future.

Cradling her rather limp sated body against him, he dried them both off, left his clothes and her wet T-shirt on the deck, and headed into the house.

She tucked her face against his chest as he carried her to the master bathroom and didn't look at him until he had the water heated up and tipped her head back. "Can you stand on your own, Little one?"

She nodded.

He stepped under the spray and lowered her carefully to her feet, keeping both hands on her until he was certain she was steady.

When he reached for the soap, she finally spoke. "I can do it, Daddy."

"I know you can, Sunshine. I bet you've been showering alone and managing just fine for your whole life, but you don't have to anymore. Most of the time Daddy will wash you. Sometimes in the shower. Sometimes in the tub."

She dropped her arm and stopped fighting him. She even moaned softly as he ran the soap up her arms and over her shoulders. He kept her out of the direct stream so when he set the bar down he could massage her shoulders.

That caused her head to roll back. "Feels so good, Daddy."

"I'm glad, Little one." He eventually picked the bar back up and ran it over her breasts. Her nipples stiffened and she pushed at his hand to get him to stop.

He tipped her head back with one finger under her chin. "Let Daddy wash you. *All* of you. Be a good girl." He knew he was pushing her, but it seemed important that he chase the demons from her head, and the best way to prove to her it was okay to feel sexy and aroused right now was to keep her that way.

"Grab my shoulders," he demanded as he squatted in front of her to wash her feet and legs and finally her pussy. When he reached back farther to pay special attention to her tight little rosebud, she rose up onto her toes and squeezed her cheeks together. "Daddy..."

"Lower your feet, Sunshine. No part of you is off limits to Daddy. Not even inside your bottom. I'm not going to stretch out your tight little hole tonight, but I will soon."

She shuddered, a soft noise coming from her. He smiled to himself, knowing he had turned her on with his promise.

After removing the nozzle so he could thoroughly rinse her off between her legs, he guided her to the built-in tile bench seat. "Can you sit here for Daddy while I wash myself?"

She nodded and sat on her bottom. She also watched him, squirming while he faced her the entire time he soaped his body and then paid special attention to his fully erect cock. His erection seemed to have forgotten that just half an hour ago it had been to heaven.

He certainly wouldn't be taking her again tonight, so his cock needed to stand down.

"Can I touch you, Daddy?" Her soft voice startled him, and he glanced at her to find her looking up at him with wide imploring eyes.

Damn, he was wrapped around her finger already. How would he ever be able to tell her *no*? He stepped closer and released his cock, setting his hands on the wall behind her to brace himself for her touch.

She sat taller, seemingly regaining her strength as she stroked up his length. "Is this okay?"

"Yes, Sunshine. Anything you do is more than okay."

"Anything?" She glanced at him, her cheeks rosy.

"As long as you don't use your teeth for more than a graze and you're gentle with my balls, yes."

"Can I lick it?" she asked next.

He wasn't sure where her headspace was, waffling between her Little and her adult. He was afraid she needed to be Little Jordi for the rest of the evening, so he stepped back. "Another time. You're exhausted tonight. Let Daddy finish off. You can watch."

She seemed pleased by that idea and sat with an open mouth and wide eyes while he gripped his length and gave it the few tugs it needed before his orgasm shot from the tip.

Jordi looked pleased, grinning when he finished. "Next time I want to do that," she declared.

He groaned. "You seem to have a long list of things you want to do, Little girl."

She nodded.

He rinsed off, turned off the water, and grabbed two towels. After fully patting his Little girl dry, he wrapped her up and guided her out of the shower. Keeping a close eye on her, he dried himself next and hung the towel on the rack.

Stepping out, he unwound her towel and used it to soak up more of the moisture from her hair. "Sit on the toilet seat so Daddy can comb through the tangles, Sunshine."

"Naked?" she asked incredulously.

"Yep." He wanted her to get used to being naked in front of him. Not just naked, but he didn't intend to give her much privacy at all, not even to use the toilet she was now sitting on.

After carefully working through the tangles, he took her hand and led her to the sink. He found a new toothbrush in the drawer, put paste on it, and handed it to her so they could brush together.

"Are you really going to spank me, Daddy?" she asked in a very Little voice when they were done.

"Yes, Little one. Right now. I wouldn't be a very good Daddy if I didn't discipline you when you misbehaved, would I?"

"I guess." She looked up at him. "The Daddies in books always spank the Little girls." She'd told him that once before. Apparently she read a lot.

"Yep."

"Will it hurt?" she asked as he guided her to his bed.

"Yes. Not more than you can handle. Just enough to remind you to think twice before you lie to Daddy again."

"I won't lie again, Daddy."

He chuckled. "Sometimes you will, Little girl." He lifted her up onto the bed. "On your tummy."

She rolled onto her belly but turned her head to face him. "Why would I do something that will get my bottom spanked?"

"Because you're going to enjoy it."

She gasped. "That doesn't seem likely."

He lifted a brow. "Do the Little girls in your books enjoy getting their naked bottoms spanked?"

She sighed and dropped her head. "Yeah, but that's just books. It's fiction."

He smiled. He loved how she could pick and choose what parts of her books must be real and what parts must be fiction. She was about to find out.

"Hands at the small of your back. Daddy is going to hold them so they don't get in the way. I don't want to accidentally swat your hands."

"Ugh. They do that in books too," she murmured.

He worked hard not to laugh as he gripped her wrists together and palmed her bottom. "Since this is your first spanking, I'm going to go easy on you. Ten swats. They won't be gentle, but I only want to pinken your skin tonight. Next time you can expect more."

Another sexy whimper.

Callen watched her closely as he swatted her bottom just hard enough for it to sting but not hard enough to make her cry. He loved the way she bucked and flinched, trying to get away from his palm.

When he was done, he turned her over, picked her up, and held her in his arms. "So proud of you," he said as he kissed her neck. When he was certain she wasn't deep in subspace from the brief spanking, he pulled the covers back and settled her near the center of the bed, tucking her in tight. "Be right back."

Callen pulled on a pair of shorts before backtracking through the house to turn off all the lights. He stepped outside to put the lid on the hot tub, turn down the temperature, and grab their clothes. After dropping the garments in the laundry room, he moved her clothes to the dryer, checked that the doors were locked, and returned to his Little girl.

He hadn't been gone long, but she was sound asleep.

Apparently they wouldn't be discussing everything that had happened this evening, but that was okay. It wasn't late. They could wake early before either of them needed to be at work and talk then.

Callen climbed under the covers, pulled his sleepy girl into his arms, and spooned her. He couldn't stop smiling as he inhaled her sweet scent and thanked his lucky stars.

He'd finally found his Little girl.

Chapter Ten

Jordi jerked awake, her heart racing as she tried to remember where she was. She was too warm. Arms were around her, and she was naked.

Then she remembered, and her heart rate calmed.

"Hey, Sunshine." Daddy rubbed her arm and threaded his fingers with hers between her breasts. "You must have slept hard. I know I did."

"I think so." The rest of her memory flooded back. She twisted around, sat up, and looked down at him. When she remembered she was naked, she grabbed the sheet to hold it in front of her. "I'm naked. We had sex. Oh, God. I climbed on your lap and, and, and..."

Her face heated.

Her Daddy chuckled as he reached for her. "Calm down. You say all that as if you were drunk and regret it." His face fell a second later.

She shook her head and tried to think how to reassure him. "I don't regret it. I'm just...remembering...and I'm embarrassed."

He tugged the sheet out of her grip, baring her chest to him.

His fingers came to her nipple and circled it. "No reason to be embarrassed. I want you to be comfortable with me, Little one. Naked and exposed. All our faults bared."

"You don't have any faults," she blurted.

He smiled. "I'm sure I do. You just haven't discovered them yet."

"Have you discovered mine?" she asked, horror flooding in.

"No, Jordi. Daddy hasn't found a single fault with you. You're precious."

She felt odd. She hadn't ever woken up with a man before. She was also straddling her adult and Little headspace. She bit her lip. "I don't know who to be," she admitted.

"How about you be Little right now. No sexy stuff. Let Daddy take care of you for a while this morning before we have to go to work."

"Okay." That might work. She could do that. If she didn't think about his erection and how good it felt inside her and how sexy he'd been while he stroked it and how he'd... *eaten my pussy! Oh God.*

She yelped.

"Jordi..." He looked concerned now as he sat up next to her. "Stop thinking so hard. I have an idea." He slid off the side of the bed and reached for her.

She trembled as he stood her on her feet but relaxed when he grabbed a clean T-shirt from his drawer and pulled it over her head. She was glad he was wearing shorts.

"Go potty, then I have something for you to see."

"What is it, Daddy?" she asked as she squeezed her legs together. She really did need to pee.

He pointed toward the bathroom.

She hurried to do as he told her, closing the door almost all the way while she rushed to empty her bladder and wash her hands. When she was back in the room, she found him standing next to a door across from the bed.

"What are you doing?" she asked as she approached.

When she reached him, he cupped her face and tipped her head back. "It's very early," he reminded her. "I want you to let yourself be Little for a few hours."

"Okay." That she could do. She could ignore all the adult things she'd done last night and be Little. It wasn't that she felt like she'd made a mistake. She knew that wasn't true. It was just that it had been so long since she'd been with anyone and never with that level of intimacy. He'd shown her something new and vulnerable, and it was kind of scary. What if this didn't work out after she'd let him into her heart?

Daddy turned her toward the closet door next to him. "Open it."

"What's in there, Daddy?" Wouldn't it be just clothes and shoes?

"Open it and find out."

After twisting the handle, Jordi pushed the door open to reveal a large dark area. It looked way bigger than a closet. She took a step back, unsure of what he wanted her to walk into. Callen reached past her to flip on the lights. Pale pink walls led into a room unlike anything she'd ever seen.

Jordi stepped inside and turned in a circle to see everything. "What is this place?"

"It's your nursery, Little girl."

"My nursery? How many other Little girls have shared this room?" she asked, suddenly very jealous.

"No one, Sunshine. I started putting this room together when I moved in two years ago. I haven't had a Little girl since I've lived here. I've been too busy with opening the store and establishing a loyal customer base."

Reassured, Jordi looked around again. "Can I touch things?"

"Of course. I hope you will enjoy playing in here."

Walking forward, Jordi trailed her fingers over the railing on the large crib. "This looks like it was built for me."

"It was. Let me put the side down and you can crawl

inside," he suggested as he moved forward. "There. See if you think it's comfortable."

"It's high. I think I need a stepstool to climb up there," she said, running her hand over the mattress.

"How about a boost from your Daddy," he offered.

In a flash, she sat inside. "Oh, look!" Jordi scooped up a small stuffed mouse who had sat in the corner waiting for her to find him.

"Fromage has hoped a Little girl would adopt him for a long time."

"Fromage? Is that French? It sounds fancy," she questioned as she straightened the mouse's jaunty bowtie.

"*Mais, oui, mademoiselle!* Fromage is his favorite food. He likes it so much that I started using that for his name. Can you guess what Fromage likes to eat?"

"Cheese?" she guessed.

"*Exactement!*" Callen praised her in French, making Jordi giggle with his silly accent.

"I like the name Fromage. It suits him. I can lie down in here and stretch out all the way," she demonstrated and could just touch the tips of her fingers and toes on the wooden crib. "Am I going to sleep in here the next time I spend the night? You know... If I get invited to spend the night again."

"You will be here with your Daddy as often as you'll let me steal you away from your place. I like having you here. Look, there's a place for you to play, and I even added a TV so you could watch a princess movie if you wanted to in here."

"That's fun! Where did you put the remote?"

"The remote is in Daddy's nightstand. I'll get it out for you when you have permission to watch a show," Callen said firmly.

"I have to get permission?"

"Yes. Just in case you'd make a poor decision like watching TV instead of taking a nap."

"I don't like naps."

"That will change. Little girls need lots of rest."

Crossing her arms over her chest, Jordi was prepared to argue with him when she noticed a rocking horse at the side of the room. She pushed herself out of the crib and dashed over to run her hand over the saddle. "Do I get to ride on this?"

"Yes, Sunshine. I thought you might like to be a cowgirl sometimes instead of a princess."

"A cowgirl needs a hat," burst out of her mouth before she could stop it. "Sorry, I wasn't asking for stuff."

"You simply state the truth. A cowgirl *does* need a hat."

Callen opened a door to display a small closet. On the shelf at the top were several types of hats. Before she could figure out what everything was inside, he picked up something brown from the shelf and closed the door. Her Daddy turned around, plopped the hat on her head, and stepped back to see what she looked like.

"Well, miss, I declare. You're adorable," he said with a southern drawl that made her giggle.

"I want to see!" she demanded, bouncing up and down on her toes.

"Alright. Let's go look in the bathroom mirror," Callen suggested, offering her his hand.

Skipping at his side, Jordi clung to his hand. She touched the brim of the hat and patted it down a bit more securely on the way. Hats were so much fun.

"Whoa, Sunshine."

Not paying attention where she was going, Jordi almost ran into the door frame, but her Daddy saved the day by guiding her through it safely. Catching a glimpse of herself sporting the cowboy headgear, Jordi clapped her hands in delight.

"I do look like a cowgirl!"

"A very cute one," Callen agreed. "You have just enough time to take a quick ride on the horsey before you need to get ready for work."

"What time is it?" she panicked. She hadn't even thought about work.

He pointed to the clock and she relaxed. "I have about an hour. You scared me."

"You have plenty of time for a quick ride, breakfast, and a snuggle with Daddy."

"I don't ever eat breakfast."

"You do now. Little girls need fuel for their bodies. Especially when they work as hard as you do," he corrected.

"I don't like breakfast."

"So we find something you do like. How about a smoothie?"

"Who wants to drink their food?"

"A bowl of cereal?

"It gets too soggy." she pointed out, wrinkling her nose.

"Eggs?"

"Yuck! No way!"

"How about peanut butter toast?" he offered.

"I like peanut butter."

"Perfect. A quick ride and then breakfast." When she made a face at that word, he amended his statement. "A quick ride and then some grub for the cowgirl."

"I could eat some grub. You know... as long as it's not real grubs because... gross!"

"No grubs will be injured in the making of cowgirl grub," he promised.

"Thanks, Daddy. Now, ride!"

Jordi dragged him back to the nursery and surveyed the rocking horse for a second before clambering on. She picked up the reins and held them as she rocked forward. "Whoa!"

"Careful there, Little girl. You may want to hold on to the horse's neck or the handles on the sides until you get used to the motion."

"Good idea!" Jordi wrapped her hands around the wooden pegs extending from the sides of the horse's head and tried again. This time she rocked back and forth over and over.

"I think you've got it."

"This is fun!" she cheered. "I could ride all the way to work today."

"Five more minutes and then playtime is over until tonight."

She rode quietly for a minute before asking, "Are you sure you want me back this evening?"

"No doubt in my mind. I'd keep you here in the nursery to play all day long, but we both have things to do out in the world," he lamented.

"I like the nursery."

"I'm glad. Fromage is happy you're here now, too."

"Do you think he'll understand that Norwood is my best buddy? I mean, I'll like Fromage a lot, but Norwood's been with me for a long time."

"Fromage knows there's plenty of room in a Little girl's heart for two stuffies. He's looking forward to meeting Norwood. They may be best friends soon since they both love the same Little girl."

"Fromage can't love me, silly. We just met."

"There's not a time requirement for love, Little girl. It comes to surprise us sometimes."

She rode silently for several rocks before saying, "Daddy? Do you think you'll ever love me?"

"I'm already falling in love with you, Jordi. I hope you're feeling that way as well."

Brushing her fingers through the horse's mane, she nodded slowly before peeking up at the man standing beside her. "I've never felt like this before. It's kind of scary."

"Come here, Jordi. I need to hold you." Callen helped her off the rocking horse and wrapped her in his arms. Holding her tightly against his body, he rubbed her back to comfort her. "We'll figure this out together, okay, Sunshine?"

"Okay. I'll be brave for you, Daddy."

"I appreciate that. If you get scared, tell Daddy so I can help."

"I promise."

Chapter Eleven

Arriving at work, Jordi dug into the next tasks on her list. Everything was coming together, and she was so pleased by the result. Checking her schedule, Jordi was glad to see that she was still ahead, thanks to her Daddy's help in getting a ton of small tasks done. She rolled up her sleeves and got started.

When her phone rang, Jordi was surprised to see she'd been working for several hours. Usually, she stopped in the mid-morning to have a snack but her stomach hadn't growled once. *Must be due to that grub.* She was laughing as she answered the phone.

"Hi, Daddy!"

"Hi, Sunshine. I've got an idea for you. How would you feel about having a play date with another Little this evening? We could go out to dinner first to get to know the Little girl and her Daddy before you play."

Fright flowed through her like an icy river. "Daddy, I'm scared."

"This is a big step, Little girl, but I will be right there with you. Wouldn't you like to meet someone who feels like you do?"

"They'll make fun of me."

"The Little I'm thinking about is way too sweet to do that. And don't forget, I'll be right there with you," he assured her.

"Who is it?"

"Sue from Little Cakes. I asked her Daddy, Davis, how she was feeling, and she's been very blue lately. He wanted to cheer her up and didn't know how."

"Oh, no. I like Sue... So she really is Little?"

"She is."

"Can I change my mind? If I get scared at dinner?"

"Of course. You can change your mind any time you want," he assured her.

"Do you think this is important?"

"I think you need to know you're not alone or different than other people."

She hesitated for several breaths, hoping he'd say something and tell her he was just kidding or that she didn't have to do it. Her Daddy just waited patiently for her to think it through. Finally, she swallowed hard and said, "Okay."

"Good girl. Can you leave there at five?" he asked. "I can come over and help with a few tasks if you need to get ahead."

"No, I'm caught up thanks to you. I could leave at five. I was going to go to my apartment," she said hesitantly.

"I'll set up the dinner date for six so you have time to stop by your apartment, grab some clothes, and come back here for a quick shower before we need to leave."

"I could do that," she agreed.

"It's going to be okay, Sunshine. This will be fun."

"I'm still scared," she admitted.

"I know. That's okay. It's something new you haven't experienced yet. Like before you ever had a Little Cakes cupcake. You didn't know what that was going to taste like. It could have been dry and stale, but it wasn't. It was addictingly delicious, and you're so glad you tried it. You're going to love having a Little playmate just as much."

"What if I don't?"

"Then you can spank Daddy," he suggested with a snicker.

An image of his toned bottom flashed into her mind, making her drool. *I could spank that all day.* "Deal."

His booming laughter made her giggle as well. She didn't have to follow through on anything if she didn't want to.

"Hi, Jordi. So good to see you." the buff, handsome silver fox said with a gentle smile.

"Hi." Jordi didn't know what to say after that, so she looked at her feet.

A pair of pink sandals featuring purple toenails entered her view, and she looked up to see Sue standing in front of her. "Hi, Sue."

"Hi, Jordi. I'm excited to spend some time with you. I don't get a lot of play time with other Littles. I cleaned my nursery and everything," Sue shared quietly so the other people standing in the restaurant entrance couldn't hear.

"You have a nursery, too?"

"I do. It's my favorite place in the house. Da... Davis and I do puzzles together and read stories."

"That sounds like fun," Jordi offered as a response, trying to feel her way through what she was supposed to say. She paused and cleared her throat before whispering, "I've never done this."

"Have dinner?" Sue teased with a smile before adding, "It's okay. Things are scary at first then you have fun."

When the hostess led them to their seats, Jordi walked through the tables filled with diners. *Thank goodness, this is a casual place.* No one seemed to notice them at all. They had no idea why the group was there.

Soon she slid into the far corner of a booth secluded in the shadows and her Daddy sat next to her on the bench seat. His hand wrapped around her thigh to give her a small squeeze of reassurance. Jordi looked across the table at Sue and attempted a smile.

"I haven't eaten here before. What do you suggest I try?" Jordi asked.

"I love the mac and cheese. It's sinfully good," Sue told her.

"They have mac and cheese?" Jordi searched through the menu to find it as Davis and Callen ordered drinks for the table.

"We don't ever have that at home," Sue said, nodding at Davis. "It's not healthy. But if we go out, anything is fair game."

"Almost anything, Little girl," Davis warned. "Ordering three desserts for dinner is not acceptable."

"You ordered dessert for dinner once?" Jordi asked.

"There wasn't anything on the menu I wanted—but they did have great pies. I ordered pumpkin and apple pies. That's almost a vegetable and a fruit. The brownie to finish off my meal is what got me overruled."

"Pumpkin is a vegetable and apple's a fruit. That makes perfect sense to me," Jordi said, backing Sue up.

"And the brownie?" Callen asked.

"I'm with Sue. You have to get dessert," Jordi stressed as she turned the menu over to look at the list of sweet things on the back.

"Food first. Then maybe dessert. One dessert," Callen stressed.

The Daddies looked over the menu with their Littles. When the waitress came back with water and tall glasses of milk for Sue and Jordi, the men ordered for their Littles and themselves. Jordi felt conspicuous and scooted closer to her Daddy. Again, he reassured her with a squeeze to her thigh.

"I love men with old-world manners. Why can't I find someone to order for me?" the waitress asked before leaving to put in their orders.

"She didn't know," Jordi remarked in shock.

"People are too busy. No one really knows anything," Sue reassured her before pointing at a couple across the aisle from them. "I like to make up stuff about people. I think those two are spies and they're in here to watch the people at that table."

Jordi followed her gestures and watched. The couple close to them did spend most of their time looking at the table Sue had indicated. They were sneaky but Jordi was able to catch them several times. "Goodness! I think you're right."

"What do you think is going on over there?" Sue asked, pointing to a different table.

Jordi watched them carefully for a few seconds and suggested, "Maybe they had a big argument before coming here. She's still totally pissed, and he's trying to calm her down."

"She does have her mad face on," Sue agreed.

Jordi squirmed in her seat as she looked around. This was fun. She knew she was wrong with every guess, but creating convincing stories was a blast.

"Here's your dinner," the server announced and set the first dish of macaroni on the table in front of Jordi. "Be careful. It's hot."

Leaning forward, Jordi inhaled the cheesy aroma of the delicious-looking dish. It was steaming. She could feel the waves of heat wafting off the dish. She picked up her fork to dive in when Callen caught her hand.

"Let it cool off a bit. You'll burn your mouth." He dipped his fork into the mixture and lifted it to his lips to blow on it. When it was cool, he offered it to her.

Accepting the bite, Jordi chewed carefully. It wasn't molten, but it was still hot. Thank goodness she hadn't popped that bite into her mouth without him blowing on it.

"Hot, huh? Did you burn your mouth?" he asked in concern.

"No, you'd cooled it off a lot."

"Good. Here. Let's put a few bites on this bread plate. A smaller amount will reach a safe temperature faster," Callen suggested.

"Smart! We're stealing that idea," Davis cheered as he followed Callen's example.

Soon everyone was able to enjoy their meal without fear that the molten sauce would sear the tops of their mouths. Jordi felt herself relaxing each moment she spent with Davis and Sue. They were obviously in love and he cared for her so easily. When Sue got a bit of sauce on her chin, Davis wiped it off smoothly before Jordi even had a chance to warn her.

Peeking up at Callen, she wondered if they would ever be that easily in tune with each other. His hand wrapped around her thigh once again to squeeze gently, making her smile up at him. Jordi didn't think she'd ever had a boyfriend who cared so much about her. Already he knew secrets about her that no one knew.

"Will you come play in my nursery?" Sue asked as they finished the delicious food.

"I'd like that," Jordi answered, feeling excited to see the other Little's special room.

"Yay!" Sue cheered and nudged her Daddy.

Davis caught the server's attention, and the men settled the bill so they could leave. Callen followed Davis back to their place and parked.

"Stay there, Jordi. I'll come let you out," Callen instructed as he turned off the car before rounding to let her out.

Walking up to the door a few minutes later, Jordi shook off the nervousness that tried to creep up her spine. *This is going to be fun!* Sue waited for her and took her hand as soon as they got inside.

"Come on. I can't wait for you to see," Sue urged.

Jordi paused at the door to the enchanting room. It looked like Sue. "This is beautiful. You are so lucky."

Jordi ran to the full bookshelf and dragged a finger over the colorful spines of the books. "You have so many books."

"Daddy is the best reader. He makes books come alive," Sue bragged.

"Now, Cherry. I'm sure there are other Daddies who excel at that as well," Davis said from the doorway.

"No way," Sue denied.

"You two play nice. We'll come in and check on you from time to time," Davis assured them.

"Thanks, Daddy," Sue cheered. "We'll be good."

"Promise!" Jordi echoed as Callen looked in.

As soon as the men walked down the hall, Jordi looked at Sue and asked, "Cherry?"

"That's what Daddy calls me. I love it. What does your Daddy call you?"

"Sunshine."

"Oooh, I like that, too. I can tell he really likes you," Sue stated firmly.

"You can?" Jordi asked.

"Of course. He never looks away. I bet he'll be the first Daddy to come down the hall to check on us," Sue forecasted before dashing over to pick up a large plastic box. "Do you like to play with blocks? I've got a bunch of these that interlock."

"I haven't played with those in forever. Here, let me help you." Jordi rushed forward to take one side of the big bin, and the two Littles carried it over to the table.

"Shall we make something together? How about a castle?" Jordi suggested, as they both took a seat.

"Neat. You'll know how to put the base together to make it last. Can it have turrets?" Sue asked, digging into the bin.

"How about three?" Jordi already had an idea in mind.

"Perfect. Wait! If we're making a castle, we need to be princesses." Sue jumped up to run to the dresser. Sitting on top were two tiaras.

Returning to the table, she looked at both and handed over a gorgeous blue one. "You have to wear this one. It matches your outfit."

"It's so pretty. Are you sure it's okay for me to wear it?"

"Of course. We're princesses!" Sue exclaimed as she set one with white stones on her head.

"I love being a princess!" Jordi cheered.

"You're a beautiful princess," Callen's voice assured her from the doorway. "You princesses doing okay?"

The two Littles looked at each other and laughed. Sue had been right. Jordi's Daddy was the first one to check on them.

Jordi stood and walked carefully to her Daddy as she balanced her tiara on her head. "Look, Daddy. I get to be a princess here, too. And we're making a castle!"

"You are having fun, aren't you? I'll get out of the way. Princesses need plenty of room to create castle masterpieces!"

"Thanks, Daddy," Jordi said and anchored her tiara on her head with one hand as she rushed back to help with the construction project.

Chapter Twelve

Waking up the next morning wrapped in her Daddy's arms, Jordi lifted her head to check the time before pressing a kiss to his hard chest. "Good morning, Daddy."

"Good morning, Sunshine. You sound happy this morning."

"I am. I had fun last night. Can I have Sue over here sometime to play in my nursery?"

"I think that's an excellent idea. The two of you had great fun together. I don't think Sue will ever take that castle apart."

"We'll build a better one next time. Maybe we could get something fun to do in my nursery?"

"I think that's a great idea. You decide what you would like, and we can do some online shopping this weekend."

"Fun!" She wiggled against him and squeaked as he pulled her tight to his body.

"You're not teasing your Daddy, are you?" he playfully growled before attacking her with kisses along her sensitive neck.

"Maybe..." she answered, drawing the word out as she traced her fingers down his powerful arm.

"You're going to be late to work," he warned as he rolled

over, pinning her to the bed with his body. His hands glided over her form, caressing her.

She loved how he seemed to sense exactly where she needed his attention. When he paused to meet her gaze expectantly, Jordi realized he was waiting for an answer. "Damn work."

"That's my Little girl."

He lowered his mouth to hers in a tender kiss that flared quickly into a heated exchange. Jordi clung to him as she explored his body—every groove, nook, and curve tantalized her.

"So hot!" she murmured when he lifted his lips.

"Combustible," he agreed before trailing kisses over her shoulder as his hand cupped her breast. When she arched her back to thrust herself into his hand, Callen captured her taut peak between his lips. Rolling and nipping, he tantalized her as he kneaded her soft mound.

"More," she begged when he released her nipple with a pop. Jordi held her breath as he trailed his fiery kisses to her other breast and repeated his attentions.

When he eased his fingers down the center of her body, Jordi bit her bottom lip to keep from whimpering from need. Her Daddy took care of that.

"I need to hear your noises, Little girl. Tell me what you feel," he insisted.

"Please!"

"Do you want me to pet this naughty pussy? You are so wet, Little girl. So responsive for me."

"Touch me. Please!"

"What good manners you have, Sunshine."

He slowly traced her lower lips and lifted his fingertip to his mouth to taste her juices. "Absolutely delicious."

"Daddy!"

"It's okay for me to enjoy you, isn't it, Sunshine?"

Jordi felt her cheeks heat. "You could enjoy me more," she dared to suggest.

"Challenge accepted, Little girl."

Callen wrapped his arms around her and turned onto his back, carrying her along with him. "Want to ride Daddy like your rocking horse?"

Eagerly, she nodded. "But I don't have my cowgirl hat."

"Go get it, Sunshine."

He helped her slide off his body to the edge of the bed. Jordi ran for the nursery and flipped on the lights. In a flash, she grabbed her hat from the closet and ran back to find her Daddy, propped up in bed waiting for her. His hand stroked over his cock as he waited.

Scrambling back onto the bed, Jordi eased herself more carefully over him. Daringly, she rubbed her pussy on his shaft, drawing a low groan from Callen.

"Let me make sure you're ready, Sunshine." He reached forward and caressed her, seeking all those sparkly spots that made her shiver. He seemed to have memorized them all.

When she wiggled, eager for more, Callen wrapped his hands around her waist and lifted her up. He shifted to place the broad head of his erection against her and drew her slowly down, controlling her descent when she would have rushed.

As their bodies joined fully, Jordi held onto her Daddy's thickly muscled arms. He felt even larger like this as if he claimed every speck of space inside her. She hesitated for a second to allow her body to adjust as he stretched her tight channel.

"Okay, Little girl?" he asked, cupping her jaw.

"Okay..." she groaned. "No, that's a lie. I'm more than okay."

Smack. His hand landed smartly on her bottom, and she bolted forward, making them both moan at the sensation.

"Did you spank me?" she demanded as she settled back down on him.

"Did you lie to me?"

"Maybe?" She hedged her bets to avoid another smack. It didn't work.

Again that hard hand landed on her bottom, making her move forward. "Daddy!" Jordi protested, rubbing the sting from her punished flesh.

"Ride me, Cowgirl. This stallion may just be a bit rough to ride," he warned, before bouncing her up and down on his shaft.

"I can tame you," she promised, giggling as he moved her once again.

Jordi launched into action, moving up and down on him. She discovered that she could move in different angles and make them both inhale sharply. Her cowgirl hat tilted and began to slip off her head. Slapping one hand over it, she rode her Daddy like he was the most buckingest horse ever.

No rocking horse could ever rival this. Jordi felt the tingles gathering together inside her. She shifted backward and forward, trying to find the exact spot she needed to feel him to climax. Callen pressed his thumb against her clit. The rough calluses of his working man's hand provided the perfect touch to help her.

"Aahhh!" Jordi cried out into the room as her body seized with a massive orgasm. She writhed on top of him as he touched her.

"That's my Sunshine," he praised. "You're going to do that again."

"Uh uh. I can't."

"Oh, yes, you can," Callen promised as he sat up fully.

Wrapping one arm around her waist, he helped her ride him faster and faster. Those sparks gathered low in her belly as he took over. Jordi slid her hands over his body, loving the gleam of sweat that formed on their skin. When Callen's free hand tapped her bottom lightly, she wiggled in response and there! Her body exploded around him, squeezing his cock buried deep inside her.

"Little girl," Callen groaned as he thrust quicker. Exploding inside her, he hugged Jordi to him as if he'd never let her go.

Jordi crossed her fingers. *Please, let this be for real. Please, let him be my Daddy forever.*

"I'm never letting you go, sweet Sunshine," he told her as he lay back on the bed, drawing her down on his chest. When the brim of her hat bonked him on the nose, he plucked it from her head and tossed it to land on the post of the headboard.

Of course, he made it. Her Daddy was pure magic.

Later, as she rushed in to finish the last remaining tasks of the remodeling job, Jordi couldn't keep the smile from her face and ended up having to wear a mask to keep the sanding dust out of her mouth. It was totally worth it.

"Jordi! It looks amazing in here," Louisa complimented.

Turning off the power equipment, Jordi pulled off her mask and commented, "It's almost ready for the full walk through. Can we schedule a time tomorrow for you to see the final product?"

"Of course. I can't imagine how it can get better. Oh, my! Look at the pipes at the sink! That is gorgeous. This is going to be an amazing place to work."

"I hope everyone loves it for years to come," Jordi celebrated. This was exactly the reaction she'd hoped to see.

Chapter Thirteen

"I'm so happy for you," Callen declared as he swung his Little girl around in a circle later that evening.

She giggled, tossing her head back and then squealing from excitement. "I did it, Daddy! That was my first really large project, and I did it. I also did it on schedule and under budget! I was worried for a few hours I would end up losing money if I had needed to move those pipes, but you saved the day with your suggestion to leave them exposed and make it look intentional. The client thought it was so cool."

Holding her around the waist high off the floor made her taller than him, and Callen pulled his Little girl's head down for a kiss. "Don't give me any of the credit, Little girl. It was all you. You would have figured out a solution by yourself. I know you would have."

"Maybe," she admitted as he let her slide down to her feet, "but I like to think we were kind of a team. That part was fun. I liked it when you came in and helped me out. Without you, I wouldn't have gotten the job done on time. My usual assistant, Paul, still hasn't been back to work. He told me his daughter had the flu earlier this week, but I haven't heard from him again in a few days. I think he might have lied and he's not coming back and he didn't have the balls to tell me to my face."

Callen frowned. "That's not very kind. How long was Paul working for you?"

"For a few weeks. He did a great job though, and I thought we worked well together, so it kind of surprises me that he would just not show up or call."

"I'm sorry, Sunshine. I guess we need to find you another assistant then. I'll keep my eyes and ears open at the hardware store. I'm not currently hiring, but I might see an application for someone who would be perfect for you."

She hugged his neck really tight. "Thank you, Daddy. That would be amazing."

"Do you already have your next job lined up?"

She nodded, grinning wide. "Yep. But it doesn't start until the middle of next week. I'll need to take some time to go over the details and gather the hardware I'll need, but other than that, I have four whole days off."

Callen lifted her hands to his lips and kissed her knuckles. "I love that. I'll make a few calls and get someone to fill in for me too. We can have four days together. How does that sound?"

Her grin widened along with her eyes. "Really? You could do that? I don't want to interfere with your job."

He chuckled. "Sunshine, it's *my* store. I'm the boss. I have capable employees. It's Friday night, and we need to celebrate. How do you feel about going to Blaze tonight? You could see lots of the other Littles who live in town and get to know them."

She stiffened. "That's very scary, Daddy. Much scarier than a night with Sue."

He squatted down in front of her, still holding her hands. "How about you think about it while we eat dinner, and then we can decide together?"

"Okay," she said softly.

He knew she was nervous, but he also suspected she would

110

be far more comfortable in her own skin and accepting of her Little once she met so many other people just like her, and Lord knew there was no shortage of Little girls in this town.

"Let's get you showered and changed before we eat." Callen took her hand and led her through the house to the master bedroom and into the bathroom.

As soon as they stepped inside, he turned on the shower so it could warm up, and then he turned to Jordi and pulled her shirt over her head. She held on to his shoulders like a good girl while he squatted down to remove her shoes and socks and then her jeans and panties. Lastly, he released the clasp on her bra.

She let out a sigh when Callen removed that last item of clothing. He knew most women felt relieved when they got home and could take off their bras, and he mentally made a note to always undress her after work and replace her adult clothes with play clothes that were comfortable and didn't require bras.

Callen stood to rearrange her hair next. It was in a high ponytail, but he carefully removed the band, twisted her hair around and around in a little bun, and then replaced the band to hold it on top of her head. "There, now it won't get wet."

She stared at him with wide eyes. "You're good at that, Daddy."

"Thank you, Little girl. Now step in," he encouraged, pointing toward the shower.

She did as he instructed, turning back to look over her shoulder. "Are you going to watch, Daddy?"

He shook his head. "I'm going to do the washing. Step under the spray to get your body wet. Be careful to avoid your hair."

He enjoyed the way her breath hitched at his declaration. He also liked how she obeyed him and stepped back toward him. With the nozzle aimed toward the far wall, he could easily wash her body without getting wet himself.

After grabbing the body wash, he poured some in his palm, rubbed both hands together, and started with her shoulders.

She closed her eyes and sighed heavily as he massaged her muscles. He bet she got pretty sore working as hard as she did every day.

He took his time, partly because she was obviously enjoying his touch but also because he was enjoying it even more. Every little moan she made caused his cock to get harder. Since he had no intention of making love to her before he got her fed, he silently instructed his cock. *Down, boy.*

Jordi held her hands at her sides while he cupped her breasts and took far more time than necessary "cleaning" them. He moved down her body next, avoiding her pussy as he made his way to her feet. "Turn around for me, Sunshine."

She quickly faced the other direction, and then rose up onto her toes when he slid his hand up between her thighs. He held her steady with his other hand on her hip while he stroked through her folds and then spent several long seconds washing around her tight little rosebud. That last part had her holding her breath.

When he was done, he removed the nozzle from the wall, rinsed her off, and turned off the water. "All clean."

She pursed her lips as he helped her out of the shower so he could dry her off. Her skin was pink from the warm water, but some places on her chest were a deeper red from either arousal or embarrassment or both. She took his breath away.

"Let's get you dressed, Little girl." He led her to the bedroom and through to the nursery. When he opened the closet, she stood next to him.

He looked down at her. "Will you let Daddy choose something for you to wear?"

She stared wide-eyed at all the selections. "All of this is mine?"

"Yep. I left the tags on in case something doesn't fit or you don't like it. Maybe over the weekend, you can play dress up and try everything in here."

Her eyes widened farther and she clapped her hands together. "Really? That would be the most funnest thing ever." She spun around and pointed at the rocking chair. "You could sit there and pretend to be the doting Daddy while his Little girl tries on clothes and then spins around for you to approve them or not." Her eyes were dancing with excitement.

Suddenly her face froze and then she wiped her smile away for some unknown reason that confused him. "What's wrong, Sunshine?"

"That was a silly idea. I'm sure you have way better things to do than watch me try on clothes." She shrugged.

He turned to fully face her, took her shoulders, and met her gaze. "No idea of yours will ever be silly, and I can't think of anything I'd rather do than watch you try on all the pretty dresses. Nothing in the world pleases me more than seeing your face light up."

She blinked as if it took her a few seconds to process his declaration, and then she threw her arms around his waist and hugged him close.

He cupped the back of her head and held her tight. She was so very precious. He already knew he was the luckiest Daddy in the world.

When she finally released him, he reached in and chose a frilly yellow dress. He'd filled this closet with mostly girly dresses with ruffles and bows and tulle and all manner of lace and pouf. She'd told him her Little was girly, so he'd gone all out.

"How about this one?"

She reached up to finger the material. "It's so very pretty, Daddy," she said reverently. "I didn't look closely at what was in the closet when I grabbed the cowboy hat yesterday morning. I wasn't ready to believe this room and its contents were real yet."

He reached up to stroke her cheeks with his thumb, one at a

time. A few tears had leaked out. He knew she'd said she was a tomboy growing up, but he felt sad for her now. Had she really not had any girly clothing and she felt like she'd missed out on something?

Callen led her to the dresser where he pulled out a pair of white panties covered in yellow sunshines.

She giggled as he squatted down to help her into them.

"Are you laughing at the panties I chose, Little girl?" he teased.

She shook her head. "No, Daddy. Never." Her eyes danced with mirth.

"Arms up, naughty girl."

She lifted them and let him slide the dress over her head. It was a perfect fit. The top fit snug across her chest with a high waistline just below her breasts that flared out into a full skirt.

Jordi immediately spun around in a circle. "It spins, Daddy."

"It sure does." He chuckled. "Better be careful so you don't fall."

"I will. Promise." She stared down at the dress, smoothing the front for a long time before looking up at him again. "I love it so much." She threw her arms around him yet again.

She was awfully emotional tonight. He wondered if something was causing her fragile feelings.

Scooping her off the floor to carry her to the rocking chair, he decided dinner could wait a few more minutes. He wanted to dig into his Little girl's mind a bit.

"It seems like you're feeling emotional tonight, Sunshine. Want to tell Daddy why?"

She shrugged and fidgeted her hands in her lap, staring at them for a long time.

He decided it would be best to wait and give her some time to think, so he rocked her gently with one hand on the small of her back and one stroking her thigh under the hem of her dress.

She finally drew in a deep breath. "It's just that there's a lot going on in my life right now, and I'm so proud of myself, and I'm really good at being enough for me." She lifted her gaze to his. "I've spent years learning to be enough for me and learning that I don't need anyone else's approval. And now you've come into my life, and you're proud of me, and you're validating my Little side at the same time, and it feels really good." Her breath hitched at the end.

Callen's chest was tight as he leaned over and snagged a tissue from the shelf on the changing table. He used it to wipe her cheeks. "The only time you've mentioned your family so far was to tell me you had three older brothers. Are you still close to them? And what about your parents?"

A red flag had gone up in Callen's mind when she'd mentioned no one was ever proud of her. That made no sense.

"It's kind of a lot. You sure you want to hear all this?"

"Yes, Sunshine. I want to hear everything there ever was to know about you," he promised.

She drew in a breath. "I'll give you the cliff's notes for now. Basically, when I was young, my life was pretty normal. Or I thought so. My parents were always busy, and my brothers were often put in charge of me. I didn't really realize until I was in my teens that all my parents ever did was fight, and suddenly they split up."

"I'm so sorry, Little one." His heart hurt for her.

She licked her lips and continued. "For a few years I didn't see my mother at all. In that time, I realized she had been the problem. Life was a bit calmer with just my father around, but we never saw him. He worked two jobs."

"That's why you spent so much time at school working with the teacher who helped you learn to love remodeling," he surmised.

She smiled. "Yes. He changed my life. But then I graduated, and suddenly my mother showed up. She ignored my brothers but thought she should step in and help me become a woman."

Callen winced. Somehow this story was going to go downhill.

"I was all set to go to school across the country to study architecture, and she thought it was a terrible idea. We fought all the time. She told me women didn't do that sort of job. It was an ugly summer that ended with my father helping me get to college several days early just to avoid her possibly trying to interfere."

"That must have been very stressful."

Jordi nodded. "It was, but at least she stopped bothering me for a while."

"So you still hear from her?" Based on her last comment, he suspected she must.

"Yeah. My father died about five years ago, and I'm not close to my brothers anymore. I never moved back to that side of the country. But my mother likes to call and text and remind me that I'm ruining my life. That I'm trying to play in a man's world, that I'll never succeed because no one will hire a woman to do carpentry jobs. I've tried to prove myself to her. I've done everything I could to make her see that I'm successful. Why can't she just love me like regular moms do?" Jordi let out a small sob and a hiccup.

Callen's breath hitched. How could anyone treat their child that way? It was disturbing. It was obvious Jordi had spent years trying to make her mother see her, and the woman apparently refused to love her daughter for who she was.

Jordi wiped her eyes and pasted on a fake smile. "But she's wrong. I can be anything I want to be. I'm successful. I just finished my biggest job to date, and I'm proud of myself, and I don't need her to be."

Callen pulled her closer against his chest and kissed her temple. "You're absolutely right, Sunshine. You've proven you can be anything you want to be, and I'm so proud of you. So very, very proud." He could be proud enough of his Little girl every day of her life that it would make up for all the years she'd tried unsuccessfully to make her mother proud.

She threw her arms around his neck. "Thank you, Daddy." When she let go, she giggled. "Can you imagine if she found out I was also Little?"

He tried to smile at her. "It's none of her business. She never needs to know." The woman was obviously toxic, and Callen would do whatever he could to protect Jordi from her. "How about from now on you come to me when you get messages from your mother. We'll listen together."

He wasn't at all sure what he would do about her mother, but he certainly didn't want his Little girl fighting battles on her own.

"Okay, Daddy. Thank you."

"Now, let's go see about dinner."

Chapter Fourteen

"What's that, Daddy?" Jordi asked when they entered the kitchen. She pointed toward the table, noticing the strange yellow seat on one of the chairs.

He shifted his gaze that direction and smiled. "Oh, that's a new addition. A booster seat. I got it today. Now you can sit up higher at the table, and Daddy can fasten you in so you won't fall off the chair."

She stared at him for several seconds and then started giggling. "I'm too old to fall off the chair, Daddy."

He gave her a mock look of shock. "Too old? That's nonsense. Little girls sometimes think they're big enough to do grownup things, but then they fall and get hurt. I would not be a very good Daddy if I left that to chance, would I?"

She sobered, shaking her head. "No, Daddy. It would be like letting me ride in the car without a seatbelt."

"Exactly." He led her over to the table, lifted her off the floor, and settled her on the seat. "See? Perfect."

She had to agree, and when he proceeded to buckle a strap around her waist, she felt even more loved and secure. Maybe the booster seat was babyish and silly, but she was learning she sometimes liked to experience really young age play. It was calming.

Perhaps she was just emotional tonight. For the entire day she'd been on the edge of tears. She'd known why too. She'd been half expecting a call or text from her mother, ruining her big day. It was silly. It wasn't as if the woman would show up. She'd never been out of the state where Jordi grew up as far as Jordi knew. She just liked to leave mean-spirited messages and texts. Jordi assumed she was a bitter old woman with nothing else to do but drag everyone down with her.

Shaking thoughts of her mother aside, she lifted her arms out of the way as her Daddy pushed her up to the table.

The room smelled fantastic. "What are we having, Daddy? And how did you get it ready?"

He winked at her as he headed for the counter. "We're having a roast. Daddy put it in the crockpot this morning on low so it would be ready tonight."

"That's so smart, Daddy." She smiled as she watched him fill their plates before bringing them to the table and returning with a sippy cup of juice for her and a glass of water for himself.

When she reached for the chubby plastic spork he'd given her, he set his hand over hers. "Give it a minute to cool off. Remember the mac and cheese?"

She nodded. "Yes. You were right. It was too hot to eat. I was lucky you stopped me from burning my mouth."

He smiled. "Daddies know these things. I'll always try to make sure you don't get injured, Little one."

She looked up at him, a sudden thought filling her with concern. "Except when I'm at work, right? You wouldn't interfere with my job or ask me to be Little while I'm working, would you?"

"Never, Sunshine. You have my word. Your job is your domain. Any time you want Daddy to provide advice or help you lift heavy things or step in when you're shorthanded, I will be there for you, but I would never suggest you can't run a business, nor do I believe remodeling is a man's job." He set his hand over hers and gave a reassuring squeeze.

"Okay, Daddy." His words calmed her.

"That's the beauty of age play, Sunshine." He grinned. "You get to come home from all that hard work and responsibility and turn your care over to Daddy. You get to be my Little girl when you're not working. Your Little wears pretty dresses and bows in her hair. She's far too young to touch hot stoves or sit on big-girl chairs. Sometimes she needs a sippy cup and a plastic plate."

Her heart felt so much better. He understood.

He leaned in closer, still holding her hand. His voice was lower when he added, "Sometimes your Little will want to spend time even younger and submit even deeper to Daddy with bottles and diapers and pacifiers."

Her breath hitched. If she was honest with herself, she'd admit she'd seen piles of diapers under the changing table in the nursery. Like the closet full of clothes, she hadn't let herself dwell on that fact for even a second. She'd focused on the rocking horse and the cowgirl hat, the crib, and Fromage the mouse. Nothing else. She had been too overstimulated to ponder the rest.

"Don't you worry, Sunshine. You'll know when you're ready to spend some time in a younger headspace. Daddy will see the signs too. We'll cross that bridge when we come to it."

"Okay, Daddy," she whispered. She was filled with uncertainty, but she didn't need to face any of that tonight. In fact, she sat up taller and made a decision. "I think we should go to Blaze tonight, Daddy. I think it will be fun."

He gave her another of his proud-Daddy smiles. "I think that's a great idea." He pushed to standing. "I better grab a bib. We don't want to get roast on your dress before we go out tonight."

Jordi's eyes were wide as saucers as her Daddy led her to the daycare section of Blaze. She'd clung tight to his arm and hidden her face as they'd walked through the club, not looking around at all the scary things she knew were in the main room. She'd seen enough as they'd stepped inside.

Daddy patted her hand where she gripped his bicep. "See? This section of the club is dedicated to Littles. The only thing in the daycare is fun stuff to play with."

She glanced at him. "I don't have to do any of those things in the main room, right?" She shuddered as she tried to block out the chains and handcuffs and benches and crosses and so many other things. Those things were for adults. She certainly wasn't judging anyone who enjoyed being strapped down and flogged, but she was far too Little to do anything like that.

"No, Sunshine. Blaze caters to many kinks. Your kink is age play. Daddy won't ask you to visit any other parts of the club. But if you're ever curious and you just want to be educated, let me know, and I'll show you around."

"Okay." She didn't think that would ever happen, but at least he'd left her the option.

"Jordi?" The sweet voice calling out Jordi's name sounded familiar.

Sure enough, when Jordi turned to see who was speaking, she was shocked to find Valerie skipping toward her. Jordi really shouldn't have been shocked. She'd wondered if Valerie and Grayson had had a Daddy/Little relationship when she'd remodeled their office a few weeks ago.

Jordi hadn't shared her kink with them at the time. She'd barely realized there might be other people who felt like her out in the world. *My, what a difference a few weeks makes.*

Valerie threw her arms around Jordi, giving her a big hug before releasing her and jumping up and down excitedly.

Grayson had followed his Little girl and was just catching up when Valerie looked back at him. "See, Daddy? I told you I thought Jordi was Little."

Jordi gasped. Her face heated so fast she thought she might faint.

Callen grabbed her around the waist to steady her.

"*Valerie*," Grayson reprimanded.

Valerie's eyes went wide with horror. "Oh, my God. I'm so sorry. I didn't mean to insinuate anything you said or did gave you away. I'm sure the only people who would ever suspect you might be Little would be other Littles themselves. We tend to have Little radar."

"Or," her Daddy challenged, setting his hands on Valerie's shoulders from behind, "you just think everyone is Little now that you've discovered the benefits of the lifestyle for yourself. Or..." he continued, "...you just *wish* everyone were Little because you're so happy and you think everyone else would be too if they would just embrace their Little."

"Yeah. That's it. I mean both of those things are right. I'm sorry for making you panic, Jordi. I hope you can forgive me."

Jordi was still stunned, but she took a deep breath and let it out slowly. After all, hadn't she done the same thing? She'd thought maybe Valerie was Little when she'd met her too. Maybe Jordi already had Little radar too.

Callen pulled her in closer and kissed her temple. "No need to worry, Sunshine. Valerie is right. Littles do tend to magnetically attract other Littles. We Daddies have Little radar too. After all, I found you, didn't I?"

She looked up at him. "I guess so."

"Don't fret. No one outside of the age-play community has any idea. Your secret is safe. Furthermore, this club is a very safe place to play with like-minded friends. What happens at Blaze, stays at Blaze."

"Okay, Daddy."

"Now, why don't you go with Valerie. I bet she'll do a better job of showing you around than I could, and she knows the names of the other Littles better than me."

Jordi hugged her Daddy close for the millionth time

tonight. He was her rock. He fixed everything. Even when she panicked. He could talk her off any ledge. She thought she might be falling in love with him, and that was scary.

Valerie reached out a hand. "Come on. I promise it will be so much fun. I'll give you a tour of the daycare and then we can play a game with some of the other Littles."

Jordi looked back at her Daddy as she let Valerie lead her deeper into the room.

He smiled. "I'll be right here the entire time, Sunshine. I won't move an inch."

She let out a long breath and relaxed. She knew her Daddy wouldn't let her down. Every time she checked, she would find him right where she'd left him.

Jordi was overwhelmed for a while, especially as more and more people arrived. By the time she sat at the table next to Valerie, she was still stunned. Ellie was there, as well as Sue and Tori who both also worked at Little Cakes. Daisy was there. Jordi recognized her from Daisy's Blooms but also because her Daddy was Tarson from the bakery. Tatiana was there from Maniac's Tats.

The surprise attendee who Jordi knew from the job she'd just completed was Kiki, one of the hairdressers from Shear Beauty. It seemed it was true. Half the town was Little.

Another woman Jordi knew from Little Cakes, Riley, popped in for just a few minutes because apparently she worked at the bar in Blaze too, and she was on adult duty tonight.

She met some new people too. One was named Avery, and Jordi was surprised to find out Avery was a detective. Another was named CC. She owned CC's Purrfect Coffee. Jordi had been there before, but she'd never met the owner. It was so fun finding out who in the community was also Little.

As the minutes ticked by and she continued to meet new and interesting people, Jordi realized that she was no different from any of these other women. They all had jobs. Several of them owned their own businesses. They spent their days in the adult world doing whatever career choice they'd made for them-selves. At night and on weekends, they submitted to a Daddy who helped them escape adult responsibilities and enjoy the fun parts of life.

The group decided to play an easy board game with colors for spaces. Jordi loved how they each encouraged each other while being competitive. It was the perfect mixture to create fun. Jordi was almost the first one to the end when Daisy rushed in to land on the final space.

"I never win!" Daisy cheered and stood to do a celebration dance.

Jordi spotted her underwear and giggled. Daisy's had small yellow flowers clumped on the fabric. Without thinking, she blurted, "Does everyone's Daddy buy them panties that match their nicknames?"

Daisy lifted her skirt to look and giggled. "I forgot. Daddy did dress me in my daisy undies."

"I've got kittens," CC piped up.

Jordi clapped her hands. "That matches your cat café! Who else?"

Rose slowly raised her hand and stood to inch her ruffled shorts down. "My Daddy calls me Rosebud. He just found these. They're tiny rosebuds. I love them so much," she shared, rubbing the soft material.

"We're all showing our panties?" a voice asked from the doorway. When everyone turned to see Ellie, she handed off a tray of cupcakes to her Daddy before tugging her dress up to reveal a pair of ruffled bloomers with cupcakes all over them.

"Your Daddy found cupcake underwear for you?" Rose asked as she admired the fun fabric.

"I did. It took finding a specialist who created them for us. Totally worth it," Garrett, Ellie's Daddy reported.

"They have people who make cute things like that, special for Littles?" Jordi asked in amazement.

"Of course!" Ellie assured her. "Just like I make cupcakes for

PEPPER NORTH & PAIGE MICHAELS

different tastes and you remodel places to make them perfect. Speaking of... I brought an assortment of cupcakes for everyone. Ready for snack time?"

Cheers filled the air, and the Littles hurriedly put away the finished game so they could eat their treats without getting crumbs on the colored board. Garrett set the platter down on the table and handed out small paper plates and napkins, decorated with the Little Cakes logo.

"Dig in, Littles," he urged.

Everyone took their favorites. Jordi waited until all the Littles had their choice before she snagged the Caramel Drizzle. Not wanting to leave her Daddy without a cupcake, she called his name.

"Daddy?"

Immediately all the men turned to look at her. The entire group burst into laughter. Daddy was a very popular name.

"Daddy Callen," she amended. "Want to split a cupcake with me?"

"How sweet of you, Sunshine. How about if I take a bite?" he asked, standing behind her.

"Okay. Here," Jordi agreed, raising it into the air for him.

Callen took a big bite and chewed, humming his delight. When Jordi giggled, he asked, "What? Do I have frosting on my nose?"

"Yes, Daddy. And caramel sauce."

Leaning down, he asked, "Can you help a Daddy out? Kiss that sweetness away."

Between snickers, Jordi kissed his nose and lips repeatedly to make sure he was perfectly clear of any traces of frosting and drizzle. "All done!"

"Thank you, Sunshine." He handed her back the cupcake. "I appreciate you sharing your treat and helping make sure the other Daddies don't laugh at me."

"I've got your back, Daddy," she promised and realized that she did. Jordi took a bite of her cupcake to give herself time to

126

think about how much she cared for Callen. He was like the caramel drizzle on the cupcake. Her life was good, but he added the extra touch that made her enjoy every day to the fullest.

Callen smoothed a hand over her hair before leaning back down to whisper in her ear, "Are you okay, Sunshine?"

"Better than okay. I love you, Daddy."

"Put the cupcake down, Sunshine," he instructed.

Slowly, Jordi set it on the plate in front of her. Had she ruined everything? As soon as she lifted her hand away, he scooped her up in his arms and excused them from the group. Jordi clung to him as he walked out of the daycare to a quiet spot.

"Say that again," he demanded.

"I—I love you," she whispered.

"Sweet, adorable Little. I'll need you to repeat that a million more times—but when we're alone so I can do this."

Callen captured her lips and kissed her over and over until she lost track of where they were and just focused on her Daddy. When he finally lifted his head, Callen told her, "I love you, too, Jordi Cross."

That, of course, triggered her pressing kisses to his lips. By the time Callen returned Jordi to her seat to finish her cupcake, the others had already thrown away their wrappers. Jordi pressed her fingers to her lips, hoping to hide her kiss-swollen mouth.

"K-I-S-S-I-N-G!" several littles chanted, teasing her good-naturedly.

"My cupcakes are so delicious they spark spontaneous kissing!" Ellie crowed, raising her arms over her head in a V of victory.

"Especially the Caramel Drizzle," Jordi agreed with a smile.

"Red Velvet!" Riley chimed in.

"Santa's Kiss!" Rose said, making kissy noises.

"Pumpkin Spice," CC cheered.

All Littles named their favorites except Sue. When everyone

looked at her, she pointed out, "Black Forest puts the cherry on top!" Everyone laughed at her finishing touch.

Jordi polished off the last bites of her cupcake as she let their chatter drift around her. She felt like she was floating above her chair. *My Daddy loves me and I love him.*

By the time she tuned back toward the activities around her, Jordi discovered everyone was coloring. Sue passed her a coloring book and a pack of crayons. Smiling her thanks at her friend, Jordi opened up the coloring book and selected a picture of a big tree to decorate. It would look perfect on her Daddy's refrigerator.

Time flew by, and before she knew it, Callen was leaning over her from behind. "Are you ready to go home, Sunshine?"

She yawned, realizing she was indeed exhausted. It had been a long stressful week, and the last few hours had been a whirl-wind of revelations that left Jordi's mind spinning.

She handed her picture to Daddy. "Can we take this home?"

"Yes, Sunshine. I'll stick it on the fridge." He took her hand and helped her stand. "Tell everyone goodbye. You can see them again another day."

Jordi rushed around the table, hugging all her new friends and the ones she'd already met before but now saw in a new light. She felt lighter and happier and excited about her kink as she skipped toward the entrance next to her Daddy, secure in the knowledge that he loved her.

After he fastened her seatbelt in the car and started up the engine, she turned toward him. "Thank you, Daddy. That was the best evening of my life. I feel so much better about myself. Just knowing there are so many other people out there like me makes all the difference."

He reached for her hand and gave it a squeeze. "I'm so glad, Little one. I'd hoped you would feel that way. Sometimes knowing you're not alone can be life changing. It sounds like you've been mostly alone for a long time."

She nodded. "Now I have you." After a pause, she added, "Right? Are you really in my life for good?"

"Absolutely, Jordi. Forever and ever. I have no doubts about being your Daddy. Now, let's get home and get you into bed. It's been a long day. Tomorrow we can sleep late and be lazy. How about pancakes for breakfast, and then we'll spend the entire day exploring your nursery and trying on all the pretty dresses."

"That sounds like it might be so much fun that tomorrow will become my new favorite day ever, and then today will be number two."

She couldn't stop grinning all the way home. Or at least she thought she had a smile plastered on her face all the way to Daddy's house. She didn't really know for sure because she fell asleep before they got there.

Chapter Fifteen

"Sunshine? We're home," Callen said softly as he unbuckled her seatbelt and untangled it from her slouched, sleeping position.

"Home?"

"Yes, Jordi. We made it home."

"I need to go to the bathroom, Daddy. I didn't go all night and we drank all that juice," she said urgently, struggling to get out of the car to run inside.

"Wait, Little girl. You're going to get tangled," Callen warned as she threw herself out the door.

With a cry, Jordi tumbled to the concrete. The jolt caused her to lose control and she wet herself. Unable to stop the flow, she soon sat there in a puddle as her Daddy unwound the seatbelt from her ankle. Completely embarrassed, Jordi sobbed, "I'm so sorry. I'll clean it up."

"Sunshine, you're okay. Accidents happen," Callen soothed. "Is your ankle okay?"

"Yes," she wailed. "But I'm sitting here covered in pee!"

"Daddy will get it cleaned up soon. Here, Sunshine, let's get you on your feet." Callen stood and lifted Jordi to her feet. He scooped her up into his arms.

"Daddy, no! You're going to get wet," she said urgently as she squirmed to get down.

"You do not want me to spank you before your shower. Daddies don't care if they get wet, Sunshine. I'll put our clothes in the washer tonight and everything will be clean for tomorrow," he explained as he carried her quickly through the house to the large master shower.

As he set her down on the tile, she whispered, "And the garage?"

"That concrete will clean up easily. I'll go dump a bucket of water on it when I get you in the shower. Everything will whisk down the drain," he assured her as he unfastened her clothing.

When she was undressed, he turned on the water and adjusted it to warm as she stood out of the spray. "There you go, Jordi. It's ready for you. Be careful in the shower without Daddy. I'll be back in a flash."

Walking forward into the warm liquid, Jordi turned in a slow circle, letting the water rinse her clean. She tried to brush off her embarrassment, but she was still mortified at losing control. When her Daddy reappeared in his birthday suit, having obviously dumped his clothes into the washer as well, Jordi started crying again.

"Little girl? What is this? There's no need to get upset. Everything cleaned up." He pulled her into his arms and rubbed her back as the water streamed over their bodies.

"Now you're going to be grossed out every time you see me."

"Do I look like I'm turned off by your body?" Callen asked, stepping back so she could see his erection thrusting proudly into the air.

Staring at his cock, Jordi licked her lips without thinking. His shaft jerked in response as Callen moaned.

"You're going to kill me, Little girl."

"You're really not mad."

"I'm not mad at all. Perhaps being at Blaze with all the

Littles made you feel super Little. I think you should wear a diaper next time so if you forget to go to the bathroom, you're protected," Callen suggested.

"One of those on the shelf?" she asked, thinking about her changing table.

"Those are yours."

"Could I wear one before we go—you know, just so I'll know what it feels like?"

"I think that would be a very good idea. Now, let Daddy make sure you cleaned every nook and cranny," he said, dispensing body wash into his hands.

Jordi didn't protest. She wanted to feel his touch to reassure her everything was okay. She sighed in delight as his hands smoothed over her shoulders and arms before whisking over her collarbones. When he reached her breasts, Jordi took a deep breath in and closed her eyes. Callen swirled his fingers around her tender mounds and playfully tweaked her nipples.

"Don't go to sleep, Little girl," he reminded her when her eyelids flew open so she could meet his gaze.

She couldn't break their connection as she felt him wash her abdomen and lower. He stroked over her pussy and cupped her small mound to squeeze it lightly. When his fingers dipped into her pink folds, she rose onto the tips of her toes.

"Spread your legs, Little one," he directed.

When she shifted into the position he wanted, those caressing fingers traced her lips between her thighs before he wrapped an arm around her side and cleaned between her buttocks. When she tried to squirm away as he cleaned around her small, hidden opening, Callen held her firmly against him.

"Stop," he reprimanded her sharply. When she froze in place, he dipped his finger slightly into her tight channel. The lather eased his way in but stung her sensitive tissue.

"Daddy, it burns."

"I'm sorry, Sunshine. It's important to get clean. Let's rinse you off now." She relaxed as he removed his finger and turned her into the shower spray to remove the suds.

In just a few minutes, he finished by washing her legs and then her face last. When she stood in front of him squeaky clean, Jordi smiled and shared, "I feel better, Daddy."

"I'm glad. Want to stay in here while Daddy showers?"

"Yes, please."

She chose a spot to lean against that got a bit of spray to keep her warm and a great view of his hard form. Callen rubbed the body wash into a thick lather before spreading it over his chiseled abs and chest. By the time he had washed and rinsed his torso, she was squeezing her thighs together, hoping she wouldn't be too wet when her Daddy dried her with the towel.

Jordi felt like her eyes would pop out when he gripped his cock in one hand and stroked down the length. She just wanted to feel it. Stepping away from the wall, she froze when her Daddy cleared his throat.

"Where are you going, Sunshine?"

"Um... I thought I could, you know—help you?" she stammered.

"Hmm." He appeared to think about her offer as he cupped his balls and washed them carefully. "Perhaps you could help me rinse off all the suds."

"I'd be very good at that," she promised, watching him whisk the lather between his powerful buttocks.

Callen reached up to remove the sprayer attachment from the wall. He handed it to her. "Here, Little girl. Help Daddy."

Immediately, she got to work. Spraying over his thick erection, she spotted one section of his neatly trimmed nether hair that wasn't rinsing clean. She reached a hand forward to adjust his shaft so the water would reach it better. The moment her hand wrapped around him, she couldn't resist stroking up and down.

When his hand folded over hers, she quickly looked up at

him to make sure she hadn't done anything wrong. The fire in his gaze was addictive. Could she make it blaze higher?

"Show me, Daddy?"

"Little girl," he growled as he moved their hands roughly down his shaft. "You didn't get to taste me before. Would you like to make sure all the suds are gone?"

"Yes," she said, dropping easily to her knees in front of him. Callen shifted immediately to block her from being pelted in the face by the shower. After smiling her thanks, Jordi leaned forward and tasted the broad tip. She swirled her tongue around the head, evoking sounds of enjoyment from deep in his throat. Encouraged by his obvious approval, Jordi wanted to pleasure him even more. She trailed her tongue down his cock to the root and flicked it under his shaft before gliding a path on the opposite side.

He reached down to fist his hand in her hair. Shifting to place the thick head at her lips, Callen pressed his hips forward. "Take me, Little girl."

Opening her mouth, she wrapped her lips around his erection as he glided inside just a few inches. Jordi tried to bob her head forward to take more of him, but Callen held her steady.

"Wrap your hands around the base, Sunshine. I'm too much for you to swallow."

He withdrew and pushed in again. "That much, Sunshine. Don't try to take all of me. Play."

Releasing her hair, Callen gave her permission to explore. She loved that he gave her boundaries. That erased any of her anxiety that she wasn't doing enough to please him. She experimented with kisses and tasting him.

When she wrapped her hand around his sac and tugged gently, he roared, "No more."

Callen lifted her to her feet and prowled forward to pin her against the tiles. Lifting her, he fitted his cock to her wet opening and glided inside, filling her fully. His bulk supported her without strain, and she wrapped her legs around him to make sure he didn't stop.

"Hold onto Daddy, Little girl. This is going to be fast."

After pulling out of her in one quick motion, he thrust back into her. She squirmed against him as he glided over all those special spots inside. He raised her just a bit more and changed his angle.

"There!" she cried out, not realizing she had said anything.

Electric sensations flew through her body as he moved. Her eyes closed to concentrate. His lips trailed a line of fiery kisses down the curve of her throat. When he bit and sucked gently where her neck and shoulder met, that was the last push. Jordi screamed her pleasure into the shower. The sound echoed off the tiled walls.

"Aaah!" he shouted. Their voices blended together as he emptied himself into her warmth.

When Callen finally lowered her to the shower floor, she leaned against him, overwhelmed by the magic of his lovemaking. "Daddy," she whispered.

"I know, Sunshine. We're magic together."

A short time later when they had caught their breath, he guided her back into the spray to rinse off the signs of their pleasure. When they were both ready, he wrapped her in a soft towel and belted one around his waist. Taking Jordi's hand, he led her to the nursery and set her on the changing table.

"Daddy's going to put you in a diaper for bed. That way you don't have to worry about the amount of punch you drank, and Daddy's juices will be absorbed by the padding."

He laid her down on the padded top and cleaned her pussy gently. Leaning over to grab a diaper, Callen pressed a kiss on her tummy. "Hips up," he instructed and tucked the diaper underneath her when she followed his directions.

"Good girl." Callen wrapped the diaper around her easily and secured the tapes at the sides to hold it in place. After helping her sit, he grabbed a cotton nightie. "Arms up."

As he eased the soft pink material over her head, she smiled.

"I think some warm milk would help you sleep better tonight. Will you drink a bottle for Daddy?"

"Yes, Daddy," she whispered.

"Let me go get it for you. Hop up into your crib and tell Norwood about your day. He's missed you."

Pulling her beaver to her face, Jordi kissed him before telling Norwood all the exciting things she had done that day. He was especially interested in all the great people she'd met at Blaze. Jordi yawned, pausing in her replay.

"My Little girl is tired. I'm back with your bottle. Come sit with me in the soft chair. I need to hold you."

Scooping Norwood and Jordi into his arms, Callen walked the short distance to the oversized chair and sat down. He cradled her on his lap and placed the soft nipple at her lips. "See if you like your formula, Baby."

Loving all the attention, Jordi allowed him to slip the thick nipple into her mouth, and she sucked tentatively. A warm milky mixture filled her mouth. It was delicious—rich and sweet. Jordi hummed her approval as she drank.

"Close your eyes, Sunshine. Daddy will take care of you."

Not wishing to miss a morsel of the deliciousness, Jordi tried to stay awake. Sleep won that battle and she crashed, wrapped in her Daddy's arms. Waking up a bit in the middle of the night, she felt a firm hand press on her tummy.

"Relax your muscles, Baby girl." His voice was low and caring.

Still half asleep, she followed his directions. Jordi fussed a little when he changed her diaper. But soon her Daddy returned to bed to wrap her tightly in his arms again. Jordi felt a kiss on her temple, and she crashed back into the best dreams.

Chapter Sixteen

Jordi awoke to the scent of bacon. She smiled as she blinked her eyes open. She was curled up on her side, but a pillow was blocking her view. When she tried to stretch out her legs, she realized several things. She was surrounded by pillows on both sides, something was in her mouth, and something was between her legs.

Jordi reached for her mouth first. She snagged a strange plastic ring and removed the object. *Oh*. A pacifier. Just her size too. She didn't remember her Daddy giving her that.

She did, however, vaguely remember him putting a diaper on her and then also changing it in the middle of the night. Her face heated when she recalled wetting her panties in the garage. How embarrassing. Her Daddy had told her not to worry about it. He'd said all Little girls had accidents sometimes. But she still felt awkward.

Pushing to sitting, she glanced down to see that once again her diaper was wet. Tears came to her eyes, and she let out a sob.

"Sunshine?" Suddenly her Daddy was rushing to her side. He sat on the edge of the big bed and pulled the row of pillows out of the way. "What's the matter?"

PEPPER NORTH & PAIGE MICHAELS

She squeezed her legs together, or at least she tried to as she tugged her nightie over the bulky yellow diaper.

Daddy lifted her chin. "Talk to me, Little girl," he encouraged.

Her lip trembled. "I wet myself again," she admitted.

"Oh, Sunshine, why is that making you feel sad?" He tucked his arms under her and lifted her into his embrace, cradling her in his lap.

"That's three times I didn't make it to the bathroom in twelve hours. What's wrong with me?" she cried out.

"Baby girl, it's okay. You're in a very young headspace right now. You had a busy week being an amazing business owner. You've dealt with a lot of stress all on your own. Your mind probably needed to crash and take a break. The timing is perfect. You can have the entire long weekend to be as Little as you want. Daddy will take care of everything. You don't even have to be back on the jobsite adulting until Wednesday."

She thought about his words. Maybe he was right. Being Little for four days sounded like heaven. She'd never had this sort of opportunity before. Certainly not with an actual caregiver to take care of everything.

"Okay," she whispered. "That sounds fun, but it doesn't explain how I could lose control of my bladder."

Her Daddy rose from the bed, still cradling her as he headed for the nursery. "No need to worry, Baby girl. Last night in the garage was my fault. I knew you were sliding into a younger headspace before we left Blaze. Being with all the other Littles helped you relax and be yourself. I should have encouraged you to use the potty before we left. That's Daddy's fault. It was my responsibility. I should have taken you to the potty or put a diaper on you before we got in the car."

She stared at him as he laid her on the changing table. Was there merit to what he was saying? Had she really been sliding into a younger headspace last night?

As she thought about his words, he pulled her nightie over

140

her head. As soon as it was gone, she lifted her hand to her mouth and stuck her thumb in. It was instinctive. Maybe the pacifier during the night had been soothing. Now she craved the feeling of the nipple.

Callen smiled at her as he opened a drawer on the side of the changing table. A moment later, he gently removed her hand from her mouth and held up another pacifier. This one was blue, and she giggled when he showed her the front. It had a hammer and screwdriver on it!

She was still smiling as he popped it into her mouth. "There. I knew you would think that set was cute when I bought them. Tools for my Little remodeler."

She giggled again behind the pacifier, suckling it. She'd never had a pacifier before. She'd never indulged this younger Little side of hers. But then how could she have without a Daddy? It would have been tough. She hadn't even realized she'd needed to play this young. It had never occurred to her.

Daddy gently took her wrists and lowered her arms to her sides before pulling a strap across her tummy and fastening it to the other side of the changing table. Her arms were pinned under the strap. The restraint made her breath hitch, and she suckled harder as she arched her naked chest.

Daddy patted her tummy. "When you're really young, I'll be extra careful to keep you safe. I don't want you to fall off the changing table. That's why I piled all those pillows up around you in the bed. They kept you from rolling onto the floor and hitting your head while I started breakfast."

Jordi wiggled her legs, feeling every bit as young as her Daddy suggested. It was kind of strange and scary, but he didn't seem the least bit upset by her needs, nor was he bothered by her wet diaper.

He set his palm on the thick bulk. "As for wetting your diaper, no need to fret about that either. Lots of Littles are able to let themselves relax deeper when they're wearing a diaper. Even in their sleep. A part of you was aware of the thick material between your legs, and you knew it was safe to use it."

She thought hard about his words as he stepped to the end of the table to remove the soaked diaper. Everything he said made sense.

She watched him as he parted her thighs wide and used a wet cloth to gently clean her skin. When he was satisfied, he slid a fresh diaper under her, squeezed some kind of ointment out of a tube, and rubbed it into her folds.

Jordi's pussy came fully alive from his touch, but he didn't comment when she whimpered, nor did he linger. He gave her clit a last pat and fastened the clean diaper around her. "There. I think you could use a few days of total relaxation. Let Daddy handle everything."

He unfastened the restraint and lifted her from the table to settle her on his hip as he headed for the closet.

When he opened it, she grinned and plucked the pacifier out of her mouth. "Can we still have dress-up day, Daddy?"

"Of course. I'll just pick out something for you to wear while we eat breakfast, and after we finish, we can come back in and try everything on. How does that sound?"

"What if I spill something on it?" she said as he lifted a pretty blue dress from the rack.

He hesitated. "Hmmm. Good point." He hung it back up. "Who needs clothes to eat anyway?" he teased as he turned to leave the room.

"Daddy! I need at least a shirt."

He patted her diapered bottom. "What for?" He was grinning as he took her to the kitchen.

She covered her naked breasts with both hands as he settled her on the booster seat at the kitchen table.

Daddy lowered her hands. "I've seen every inch of you, Baby girl. No need to hide from Daddy." He fastened a strap across her waist before pushing her chair up to the table.

It wasn't lost on her that he'd called her Baby girl several times this morning. She guessed it made sense. It also made her kind of tingly.

Daddy stepped away just long enough to fill a sippy cup. When he returned, he handed it to her and pulled a bib over her head. "Don't want to drip pancake syrup down your tummy. You'd be sticky all day." He took the pacifier from her fist and set it on the table.

She watched his every move as he finished making breakfast, feeling like something huge was happening here. It was amazing and exciting and scary at the same time.

Her Daddy was amazing and exciting too. He wasn't scary though. He was just perfect.

She took deep breaths as she settled into her younger headspace, accepting it as a part of her while he flipped pancakes. She recognized that he didn't mind. He had every intention of taking care of her in every way this weekend. She didn't have to worry about a thing. By the time she went back to work on Wednesday, she would be rejuvenated and ready to tackle the next project.

Chapter Seventeen

By the time Wednesday came around, Jordi was a new person. Callen had helped her ease out of her Little space last night so she could wake up this morning and get back to work.

She loved how insightful he'd been and how he'd known exactly what she'd needed. Spending almost four days at a younger age had let her mind relax. She'd done nothing but try on all her pretty clothes, do puzzles with Daddy, watch cartoons, and play with her dolls.

When she'd been hungry, he'd fed her. Sometimes he'd rocked her and given her a bottle. She'd taken naps in her crib. She'd used a diaper. She'd grown to love the pacifiers.

Callen had left early for the hardware store this morning. As Jordi had stood in front of the bathroom mirror, she'd worried about her ability to transition, set aside her pacifiers, and put on her remodeling hat. As she'd dressed herself in jeans and a shirt with her logo on it over adult panties and a bra, she'd taken deep breaths and known she could do this.

She looked forward to building a deck at Nicoya Stevens' house. She'd been impressed by the detective when she'd met her to discuss the job. Nicoya took her job very seriously. Jordi suspected a great place to relax outside would be perfect for her.

PEPPER NORTH & PAIGE MICHAELS

The materials would all be delivered this morning. Remembering that Paul, her sometimes assistant, hadn't shown up the last two times, Jordi decided not to text. She needed to talk to him directly. Picking up her phone, she dialed his number. When he didn't answer, she left him a message.

Paul? This is Jordi Cross. Could you give me a call back? I've got a job starting today that I'll need some help with. I still have you on the schedule. Let's talk about your availability.

An hour later as she was preparing to head over to the detective's house, he still hadn't responded. She shook her head. This was so unlike Paul. He was dependable to the core. She called again. Reaching his voicemail, Jordi left another message.

Paul? This is Jordi Cross again. I'm really worried about you. Give me a call back?

Finally, her phone buzzed.

Look, Jordi. I don't play games. I appreciated the jobs you threw my way. I thought we worked well together.

Her fingers jumped over the keys as she hurried to answer him.

Paul. What's going on? I'm still counting on your help in my future projects. Please answer my call so we can talk!

Once again, she selected his number and tried to connect. The phone rang four times before he answered.

"Yes." His tone was harsh.

"Paul. What's going on? Is your daughter okay?"

"Daughter? I don't have a daughter. Your secretary canceled

the last two jobs at the last minute. I could have worked those days and earned some money on other projects if you'd given me some notice," Paul said in a disgruntled tone.

The hair on Jordi's neck stood on end. What was going on here? "I don't have a secretary. Paul, I'm just a one-person remodeler."

"I can't help you there. A lady called me and canceled the jobs. She identified herself as your secretary."

"Paul, I'm going to get to the bottom of this, but I assure you I don't have a secretary, and I didn't cancel the jobs. Someone is messing with our conversations."

"Why would anyone do that?" he asked, his voice losing its harshness.

"Someone who wants me to fail apparently. It sounds like one of my competitors has my schedule. Someone's trying to cause me to not meet my deadlines. Don't believe anything someone says unless you talk to me directly," Jordi urged.

"I'll give you one more shot," Paul agreed.

"Thank you, Paul. Can you meet me this morning still?"

"I'll be there in an hour."

Jordi arrived early to meet the truck. She started unpacking with their help as she watched, hoping to see Paul arrive. A few minutes later, he pulled up to the curb.

"Hi, Paul."

"I'm supposed to be here, right?" he asked, unsure.

"Yes. Why? Did you get another call?"

"Actually, I texted the number myself after I spoke to you."

"You did? Why?"

Paul shrugged. "To see what would happen. I said I wanted to confirm this morning's job."

"And?" This entire situation was bizarre. Who on Earth

would be so vindictive? Jordi could only imagine a competitor, but she hadn't had a run-in with any competitors.

"And I got a text confirming that today's job had indeed been canceled." He glanced around. "That doesn't appear to be the case, considering you already have the supplies here ready to start."

"Crap! Who's doing this? I promise, Paul. I don't have a secretary," Jordi said urgently.

Paul scratched his head, his brows furrowed. "I'm sorry, Jordi. I had no way of knowing you didn't have a secretary. I did think it was strange that you kept canceling on me. I just assumed you hadn't liked my work."

"That's not true at all. You do great work. I need your help."

He gave a quick nod.

Nicoya Stevens stepped out of her house at that moment. "Problems?"

"No. Everything is great, Detective. We'll get these unloaded and get started. This deck is going to be incredible," Jordi assured her. She didn't want Nicoya to find out Jordi had a problem. She might not want a contractor who had baggage working on her deck.

"Detective? Like in the police?" Paul asked.

Jordi winced, but then realized maybe the detective could be of help.

"That's right," Detective Stevens confirmed.

"Can you trace calls like they do on TV?" Paul asked.

"I can with cause."

"There's someone calling who says they're Jordi's secretary," Paul explained.

"I don't have a secretary," Jordi rushed to explain. "But everything's okay. I'll figure this out without allowing it to affect your deck."

"Jordi, relax. I know you're trustworthy. All your clients rave about you. I don't like that someone is messing with your business and pretending to be part of your staff. Give me the number. If I have time today, I'll run it through our system."

Paul carefully read her the number and Nicoya recorded it on her phone. "No guarantees, of course. There are a lot of people who spoof their numbers to make something else appear on the screen. I'll do my best."

"Thank you, Detective," Jordi said with her heart in her throat. She hated that someone was targeting her business.

"Call me Nicoya. Now, build me a pretty deck. I need a place to hide from the bad guys and girls out there."

"We're on it," Jordi confirmed.

Working steadily through the morning, Jordi thanked Paul so many times for being there, he finally told her to stop. After that, they worked efficiently in silence like they normally did. The old deck was completely gone and the new framework was in place by midafternoon.

"Let's quit for the day, Paul," Jordi suggested. "We need to let this concrete set for the night before we move on to the next step."

"I thought you'd never get tired," he said, smiling for the first time that day.

Nicoya stepped outside just as they were wrapping up. "Hey, I'm glad I caught you. This looks awesome. That old rotting deck was dangerous."

"This new one will be so much better," Jordi agreed. "They'll come to pick up the old wood tomorrow and it will disappear forever."

"Perfect. By the way, I ran that number. It's a new account —a secondary line running off this number."

She held out a piece of paper to Jordi. A quick glimpse made Jordi's stomach twist and her heart sink as she stared at the paper she now held. "Thanks, Nicoya." Her breath hitched as it suddenly dawned on her how this had happened. It was all her fault. *Why was I so stupid?*

"I take it you recognize that number," the detective stated, obviously reading Jordi's body language.

"I do. I'll take care of this, Paul. She won't bother you again," Jordi promised.

How she got home that afternoon, Jordi didn't know. Thank goodness her truck knew the way and made the turns and stoplights automatically. Pulling into her old spot at her apartment, Jordi dropped her head to the steering wheel. Grabbing her phone, she made a call.

"Jordi? Did you finish early today? I'm already at the house. Are you heading home, Sunshine?"

"Hi, Callen." Jordi heard the flat tone in her own voice and couldn't infuse any excitement into her words. "I got bad news at work and drove back to my apartment on autopilot. I'm just going to crash here for the night. I'll come back to your place tomorrow. Take care of Norwood for me, and tell him I'll be there soon."

"Not happening, Little girl. I'll be there in twenty minutes."

The call disconnected before she could argue. Jordi dropped her head back down on the steering wheel and tried to think through what she should do. Finally, she dragged herself out of the truck and up the stairs. Thank goodness, her apartment key was on her work keychain.

Walking into the quiet apartment, Jordi realized how lonely it had been to come home every night. She wrapped her arms around her stomach as it lurched again. How was she going to explain this to Callen? What if he was mad at her? She'd made a very bad decision, and it had affected her job.

Taking a deep breath, she rushed over to her computer. First things first. There was one thing she could do to at least put a stop to the nonsense.

Fifteen minutes later, just as she was finishing the first step in reclaiming her life, a knock at the door made her jump. She'd been so focused she'd nearly forgotten her Daddy was coming.

"Sunshine? Let me in."

After racing to the door, she fumbled it open and fell into his arms. Callen didn't say a word but just held her close as he edged his way into the apartment to close the door. Scooping her up, he carried Jordi to the couch and sat down.

"Tell me what's going on, Little girl."

Suddenly the dam broke loose. She had no idea why she thought she should spend a night away from her Daddy and not talk to him. Except that she was embarrassed and humiliated, and she didn't want him to find out how stupid she'd been.

She drew in a deep breath. "Someone's been calling Paul's number and canceling the jobs I had set up for him. They're identifying themselves as my secretary."

"How long has this been going on?" Callen asked, looking concerned.

"Remember when you helped me put the beauty stations together?"

"Yes, you said your assistant's son was ill," Callen recalled.

"It was actually his daughter. Well... That's what the message said. I thought it was from Paul because it said:

"*Hey, this is Paul. My daughter is sick. I can't make it today.*"

"And it wasn't Paul?" Callen guessed.

"No. I should have noticed that the rest of our messages weren't under that number, but I was too concerned with how I was going to get things done," she admitted.

"So we need to find out who this is."

"I already know. Luckily my job this week is at the home of a police detective. Paul was quick-thinking and asked her if she could run the number from the incoming calls and texts he got."

"Would you like to share that information with me?" he asked, smiling for the first time that evening.

"It's bad."

"As long as you aren't prank calling your own employees, I think I can deal with just about anything," he suggested.

"Oh, no! It's not me." She bit her lip and stared at him, trying to come up with the courage to tell him what she'd done to create this problem. He was going to think she had no business sense or common sense at all when she told him.

Daddy rubbed her back. "Jordi?"

"It's my... My mother," Jordi admitted, dropping her gaze so she couldn't see his reaction.

A few excruciating seconds went by before Callen spoke again. "I'm not sure why you're not looking at me. I'm confused. What am I missing?"

Jordi swallowed and tentatively lifted her gaze. "It's all my fault," she blurted. "You're going to be disappointed with me and think I don't have enough brains to run my own business." She threw her arms up. "Maybe you're right. Maybe I'm not meant to own a company. Maybe I'm too stupid to be in charge of money and dates and employees and purchase orders and even tools!" She was shouting now. "Maybe I'm not an adult at all. Maybe my mother is right!"

Callen's eyes widened. "Sunshine, you know none of that is true. You're going to have to explain better about what exactly happened, but I can say you are not your mother. I haven't met her, of course, but you've shared that your home life wasn't like a fifties television family. I would never judge you for the actions of others. If she had something to do with this, it's not your fault."

"I know I'm not her. It's just so embarrassing. And it totally is my own fault." Her shoulders slumped.

"Tell me how your mother got involved."

"A few weeks ago when I first got the job for Shear Beauty, I stupidly answered the phone when my mother called. For some reason, I thought she would finally be proud of me. I had several jobs lined up, money coming in, good reviews on my website. I wanted her to be proud."

"That's reasonable, Sunshine. Everyone wants their parents to be proud of them. No matter how old we get, we still want our parents' approval." He was so calm and kind while he rubbed her back, listening to her every word.

He was...present. That was the best way to describe her Daddy. He always had time for her. He looked her in the eyes when she spoke. He thought everything she said was important and mattered. She'd never really had that before. Her father had loved her, but he'd been too busy raising four kids to sit down and look any one of them in the eye.

And her mother... What a joke. In hindsight, Jordi had never had that woman's approval or attention. At least not positive attention.

"Tell Daddy the rest, Sunshine."

Jordi sniffled and rubbed her eyes as she tried to compose herself enough to admit her mistake. "I shared my work calendar with her. I thought if she could see everything I had lined up, she would realize I'm successful."

Jordi sucked back a sob and threw herself at her Daddy, tossing her arms around his neck and burying her face in his shoulder. "Why was I so stupid?"

"Jordi Cross." His voice was firm and stern. "If you call yourself stupid one more time, I'm going to take you over my knees and spank your bottom so hard you won't be able to sit for days. You are a bright, smart, successful, spunky, hard-working business owner. Not one inch of you is stupid, and I don't want to hear that word again. Understood?"

She slowly lifted her face. Tears were streaming down. "I think I'd rather you spank me," she sobbed, and then she sat up straighter and her voice grew stronger. "I made a huge mistake. Maybe if you spanked my *stupid* ass, I could purge some of my *stupid* choices and I'd feel better," she challenged.

Callen didn't even flinch. He didn't look away. He didn't look angry. He simply carefully wrapped his arms around her and eased her tighter against his chest. He started rocking her, his palm rubbing the back of her neck.

She sobbed harder. Her anger morphed into real tears that wouldn't stop falling. She cried for the young girl who hadn't had a role model, the teenager who'd moved away for her own sanity, the adult who still couldn't do enough to make her mother proud. She cried for her bad choices and because she was stressed and because she felt so incredibly lucky to have the Daddy who was holding her and validating her every step of the way.

She cried for a long time. When she finally sucked back the last sobs, Callen lifted the corner of his T-shirt up between them and wiped her face. "That's my good girl. So brave and strong."

Brave and strong? How could he think she was brave and strong? She frowned at him through her puffy, blurry eyes.

He smiled. "You are, you know. Brave and strong. Look at everything you did all on your own. You moved clear across the country, got your degree, started a business, and made it successful by the age of thirty. How many people can do that? I don't know anyone who could have persevered under your circumstances for so many years, especially while still being torn down week after week by the very person who should have supported you."

She swallowed. That made a lot of sense.

"You should be proud of yourself, Sunshine. You're an amazing woman, and I'm so humbled and lucky that you would put your trust in me to care for you and be your Daddy."

He lifted her chin and smiled. "Now, please finish your story. Tell me what exactly you think you did that was so awful and worth all this self-recrimination."

"My calendar is online. I realized after Detective Stevens handed me my mother's phone number that she'd used my calendar to sabotage me."

"Ahh. I see. She could see your upcoming jobs."

Jordi nodded. "She could see *everything*, including Paul's name and phone number. She called and messaged him, telling him she was my secretary and that I didn't need him to come to work. She even texted *me* from an unknown number pretending to be Paul to tell me his daughter was sick. That wasn't even true."

Callen winced. "Even that part wasn't true? His daughter wasn't sick?"

Jordi shook her head. "He doesn't even *have* a daughter."

Callen's eyes widened. "Wow."

Renewed tears fell, surprising Jordi because how could she have any more tears? "See? It's my fault."

"Little girl, you could not have predicted your mother would behave with such malicious intent. You've told me before that she calls and texts, nagging you to be someone you're not. There's a huge crater between nagging one's daughter to get a different job and sabotaging her career intentionally."

"Yeah, but I shouldn't have taken that kind of risk. I'm kicking myself."

"Did you remove her access when you figured it out?"

"Yes. That's what I was doing when you arrived. I changed my password. I'm also going to need to contact every single person for every job I've done and every future job to make sure she hasn't personally reached out to any of them with lies." Her entire body sagged under the weight of that upcoming task.

"I will help you, Sunshine. Don't you worry. We'll knock that list out in no time." He lifted her chin and smiled. "At least you don't have to call your hardware supplier. And here's some promising news—I've never received a single call from your fictitious secretary to cancel an order. Maybe she didn't do more damage than we already know about."

Jordi chewed on her bottom lip for a minute, thinking about his words. He had a good point. If her mother had really wanted to fuck with her business, she could have canceled her lumber orders. The evil woman had no idea that Callen James from The Hardware and Lumber Spot was a man Jordi was intimately involved with.

"I'm concerned though, Sunshine. What your mother did was nothing to ignore. You could have been severely injured trying to do that work alone," he fumed.

"I know. I'm sure she feels that would have a positive effect. I would have to stop doing anything physical if I'd torn a muscle or worse."

"I don't want you responding to any of her calls or texts from now on, Little girl," Callen said with a dark expression.

Jordi nodded. Her Daddy was right. Her mother had crossed the line this time. "I promise. I'll show them all to you."

"Well, this was a crappy day for you, Little girl. I'm so sorry." Callen pulled her in to kiss her forehead tenderly.

That small show of love made Jordi focus on what was really important. She sat up straight and smiled at her Daddy. "You know it really wasn't a bad day. I solved the problem with Paul. I discovered and eliminated the sabotage of Cross Remodeling. We made great progress on a stellar deck that Nicoya is going to love. All in all, there were some pretty great things that happened."

"That's my Little girl. Focus on the positive."

Callen looked around the apartment and asked, "Do you need to grab anything from here to take home?"

"Home. Is that what I'm supposed to call your house now?" she asked, smiling at the handsome man.

"Yes."

"Yes? That's all you're going to say?"

"I can have movers here tomorrow. Your place is with me, Little girl."

"I love you, Daddy."

"I love you, Sunshine." He narrowed his gaze. "Just so you know, I have not forgotten the fact that you put yourself down several times. I know you challenged me because you really need a spanking to help purge all the icky feelings from today. When we get home, I'm going to spank your bottom hard enough to remind you that I won't tolerate my Little girl putting herself down."

"Yes, Daddy." She shivered, but she really did want that spanking. This was definitely one of those times when it would go a long way toward making her feel better.

Chapter Eighteen

The next hour was exhausting as Callen made them both a sandwich before helping Jordi divide up the list of everyone she'd done business with, including upcoming projects. They each placed several calls, and Jordi was beyond relieved to find out that Paul appeared to have been her mother's only target.

As Jordi ended the last call and looked at her Daddy, she felt a weight lift off her shoulders. She wasn't alone. She'd never be alone again. She had her Daddy, and he was the bestest Daddy in the world. He could fix anything.

She jumped up from where she sat on the couch and rushed toward him, throwing herself against him almost before he had a chance to open his arms. After a tight hug, she leaned back. "I need that spanking now."

He brushed her hair back from her forehead and nodded. "How about we get that part over with, then we can go get some cupcakes."

She beamed. "Really?" She pushed to standing and jumped up and down. "Cupcakes! Cupcakes."

"First a spanking," he reminded her firmly. "And don't think I'm replacing a nutritious dinner with cupcakes. When we get home from having dessert first, we're still going to eat something healthy."

"Okay." She didn't even argue as he removed every stitch of her clothing and took her over his lap. She felt a sense of calm seeping all the way into her soul even before he landed the first swat, and as he continued, she found herself relaxing further, letting the pain of his spanking ground her and remind her she was loved. So very loved.

When her Daddy was done, she was crying, but he took her into the bathroom, washed her face, and kissed her gently. "I'm so proud of you."

She was pretty proud of herself too. She'd been on an emotional rollercoaster nearly all day, worrying about her business, but she felt much better now.

She knew she still needed to deal with her mother, but right now, she just wanted her Daddy.

"Let's get you dressed so we can go to Little Cakes." He took her hand and led her into the nursery.

She chewed on her bottom lip as he shifted hangers around, wondering what he would put on her for a trip out in public. He turned around, holding up a pair of black leggings and a pink, long-sleeved shirt.

When he spun it around to show her, she started giggling. Printed on the front of it in black letters was *I can do anything you can do better*.

Daddy chuckled as he opened a drawer and pulled out a pair of panties. When he held those up, Jordi giggled harder. They were covered with hammers and screwdrivers like the pacifier he'd gotten her.

He grinned. "If all the other girls have panties that reflect who they are, I want my Little girl to have some too."

"I love them, Daddy." She couldn't wait to show her friends.

She started singing and dancing around the room, "I can do

anything you can do better." It made it difficult for her Daddy to get her dressed, but he finally managed.

Jordi was still singing as she followed her Daddy to the kitchen. Just as they were about to leave, her phone rang on the counter. She picked it up, and all the blood drained from her face. Her laughter was over.

She held it up for her Daddy to see the caller ID.

Callen took it from her, connected the call, and put it on speaker. "Mrs. Cross?"

"Who's this?" her mother demanded, making Jordi flinch.

"This is Callen James, your daughter's boyfriend."

"Boyfriend? Ha. No one would want to date Jordi. Put her on the phone," her mother insisted.

Jordi winced as a tear slid down her cheek. She pursed her lips and stood taller though, wiping away the tear. She would not give this mean woman any more of her power. Jordi was an amazing person. She had a great job and the most wonderful boyfriend a woman could ever ask for. She would not cry over the lack of love she got from her mother any longer. She didn't need her. She didn't need her approval or her love.

Callen cleared his throat. He spoke distinctly and calmly. "I have no idea what happened in your life to cause you to be so callous and cruel to your own daughter, but I won't stand for it any longer. You will not call this number again. Not for any reason. Do not text. Do not send emails. Nothing. And if you ever interfere with her business again, I will call the police and have you arrested. Have I made myself clear?"

Jordi was grinning now. Her anger dissipated and flew out the window. She felt lighter and freer and so happy as she stared at her Daddy.

Her mother gasped. "How dare you threaten me. Put my daughter on the phone."

"You won't be speaking to her again. If you try, I will change this number. Goodbye." Callen ended the call and turned toward Jordi.

She ran into his arms. "I love you, Daddy."

He held her tight before tipping her head back and meeting her gaze. "No more, Sunshine. No more stress will come from that woman. I meant what I said. If she tries to contact you, we'll change your number."

"Okay, Daddy."

He smiled. "Now, how about those cupcakes?"

"Hi!" Ellie exclaimed as Jordi skipped into Little Cakes.

Jordi really needed a hug from her friends, so she raced across the room and pulled Ellie and Sue and Tori in for a hug. All four girls were giggling and squeezing each other in seconds. They rocked so hard they nearly toppled to the floor.

When Jordi pulled back, she glanced around for the first time, grateful to see there weren't any other customers in the shop. That could have been awkward.

"I'm going to lock the door," Tarson declared as he emerged from the kitchen.

Jordi's eyes went wide. "I'm sorry. I bet you were about to close."

Ellie grinned. "This is even better. We can close up and talk without any more customers coming in."

"You sure?" Callen asked. "We were hoping to get here in time to grab a treat, but we can come back tomorrow."

"Goodness, no," Ellie declared. "It's cupcake time!"

A male voice that didn't belong to Tarson boomed from the entrance, making Jordi spin around to see Ellie's Daddy, Garrett, coming in just before Tarson locked the door. "What's this about cupcakes?" Garrett asked.

Jordi could see his eyes were sparkling even though he was trying to look stern.

"Daddy!" Ellie raced over to hug him. "Look! Jordi and

Callen showed up just now. Can we all have cupcakes and milk before we have to go home?"

"I think that's a great idea, Rainbow."

"Do you still have the Caramel Drizzle ones?" Jordi asked hopefully.

Sue leaned over the display and nodded. "Yep. There's two more left."

"Excellent," Callen said. "We'll both have one." He set his hands on Jordi's shoulders.

When she tipped her head way back to look at him, he was grinning. "It's our signature cupcake, isn't it?"

"Yes, Daddy. It is."

"Certainly is easier to work with than the next special Ellie has come up with," Tarson grumbled.

Ellie giggled as she waved a hand through the air dismissively. "Don't listen to Tarson. He's just frustrated because he can't get the cherry to stay on top. It keeps sliding off the frosting."

Tarson growled, or he tried to anyway. Underneath his attempted scowl, his eyes were dancing with laughter. "Who wants to eat cherries anyway?"

"Daddy!" Daisy shouted as she emerged from the back room.

Jordi hadn't realized Daisy was even there.

Daisy skipped around her Daddy as he changed his expression to smile at her indulgently. "You just need to use a thicker frosting," she declared. "And maybe push the cherry into the top deeper." She planted her hands on his chest and rose onto her toes. "And stop complaining about maraschino cherries. Everyone knows they are the yummiest treat ever, right, girls?" She twisted around to glance at all the rest of the women in the room.

Jordi nodded with Ellie, Sue, and Tori. "I love them."

"All Littles love cherries, especially the pretty red ones that come from a jar and don't resemble a fruit at all," Sue declared.

Tori playfully slapped a hand over Sue's mouth. "Shh. Don't you dare say that in front of my Daddy. I keep trying to convince him maraschino cherries are a good fruit choice." She pealed with giggles.

A knock sounded at the door behind them, and Jordi turned around to see Tori's Daddy, Evan, and Sue's Daddy, Davis, standing outside.

Tarson hurried over to unlock the door and let them in.

"It's a cupcake party!" Ellie declared as she opened the display case. "Cupcakes for everyone." She started putting them on plates. She handed Daisy a Lemon Chiffon, Sue a Black Forest, Tori a Pink Lemonade, Jordi a Caramel Drizzle, and finally plucked out a Rainbow Sprinkles cupcake for herself.

The Daddies helped the Littles sit together around a table and brought them all cartons of milk.

Jordi turned to Ellie who was next to her and whispered, "Look what my Daddy got me." She tugged down one side of her leggings to show her the construction panties.

Ellie giggled. "Those are perfect and so cute."

When Jordi picked up her cupcake to take a bite, she met her Daddy's gaze. He was smiling at her with all the love in the world. Jordi didn't think she'd ever been happier in her life. She'd had some bad days lately, but she'd had the best, most amazing days too. She knew her mother probably wouldn't give up easily, but she also knew her Daddy would run interference and protect her.

Because Callen James was the bestest Daddy in the world, and Jordi was the luckiest Little girl who ever lived.

Author's Note

We hope you're enjoying Little Cakes! We are so excited to be working together to create this new series! More stories will be coming soon!

Little Cakes:
(by Pepper North and Paige Michaels)
Rainbow Sprinkles
Lemon Chiffon
Blue Raspberry
Red Velvet
Pink Lemonade
Black Forest
Witch's Brew
Pumpkin Spice
Santa's Kiss
Fudge Crunch
Sweet Tooth
Flirty Kumquat
Birthday Cake
Caramel Drizzle

Maraschino Cherry
Reindeer Tracks

About Pepper North

Ever just gone for it? That's what *USA Today* Bestselling Author Pepper North did in 2017 when she posted a book for sale on Amazon without telling anyone. Thanks to her amazing fans, the support of the writing community, Mr. North, and a killer schedule, she has now written more than 70 books!

Enjoy contemporary, paranormal, dark, and erotic romances that are both sweet and steamy? Pepper will convert you into one of her loyal readers. What's coming in the future? A Daddypalooza!

Connect with me on your favorite platform!
I'm also having fun on TikTok as well!

amazon.com/author/pepper_north

bookbub.com/profile/pepper-north

facebook.com/AuthorPepperNorth

instagram.com/4peppernorth

pinterest.com/4peppernorth

twitter.com/@4peppernorth

Pepper North Series

Dr. Richards' Littles®

A beloved age play series that features Littles who find their forever Daddies and Mommies. Dr. Richards guides and supports their efforts to keep their Littles happy and healthy.

Available on Amazon

SANCTUM

Pepper North introduces you to an age play community that is isolated from the surrounding world. Here Littles can be Little, and Daddies can care for their Littles and keep them protected from the outside world.

Available on Amazon

Soldier Daddies

What private mission are these elite soldiers undertaking? They're all searching for their perfect Little girl.

Available on Amazon

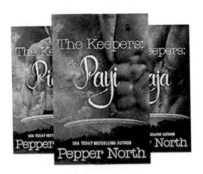

The Keepers

This series from Pepper North is a twist on contemporary age play romances. Here are the stories of humans cared for by specially selected Keepers of an alien race. These are science fiction novels that age play readers will love!

Available on Amazon

The Magic of Twelve

The Magic of Twelve features the stories of twelve women transported on their 22nd birthday to a new life as the droblin (cherished Little one) of a Sorcerer of Bairn. These magic wielders have waited a long time to take complete care of their droblin's needs. They will protect their precious one to their last drop of magic from a growing menace. Each novel is a complete story.

Available on Amazon

About Paige Michaels

Paige Michaels is a USA Today bestselling author of naughty romance books that are meant to make you squirm. She loves a happily ever after and spends the bulk of every day either reading erotic romance or writing it.

Other books by Paige Michaels:

The Nurturing Center:
Susie
Emmy
Jenny
Lily
Annie
Mindy
The Nurturing Center Box Set One

Eleadian Mates:
His Little Emerald
His Little Diamond
His Little Garnet
His Little Amethyst
His Little Sapphire
His Little Topaz
His Little Turquoise
Eleadian Mates Box Set One
Eleadian Mates Box Set Two

Littleworld:
Anabel's Daddy
Melody's Daddy
Haley's Daddy
Willow's Daddy
Juliana's Daddy
Tiffany's Daddy
Felicity's Daddy
Emma's Daddy
Lizzy's Daddy
Claire's Daddy
Kylie's Daddy
Ruby's Daddy
Briana's Daddies
Jake's Mommy and Daddy
Luna's Daddy
Petra's Daddy
Eloise's Daddies
Josie's Daddy
Littleworld Box Set One
Littleworld Box Set Two
Littleworld Box Set Three
Littleworld Box Set Four

Holidays at Rawhide Ranch:
Felicity's Little Father's Day
A Cheerful Little Coloring Day

If you'd like to see a map of Regression island where Littleworld
is located, please visit my website: PaigeMichaels.com

facebook.com/PaigeMichaelsAuthor

amazon.com/author/PaigeMichaels

bookbub.com/authors/paige-michaels

Afterword

If you've enjoyed this story, it will make our day if you could leave an honest review on Amazon. Reviews help other people find our books and help us continue creating more Little adventures. Our thanks in advance. We always love to hear from our readers what they enjoy and dislike when reading an alternate love story featuring age-play.

Printed in Great Britain
by Amazon